# FIND ME

# FIND ME

## TAHEREH MAFI

**HARPER**

*An Imprint of HarperCollinsPublishers*

ISBN 978-0-06-290628-1

Typography by Ray Shappell
22 23 24 25 26  LBC  16 15 14 13 12

First Edition

# CONTENTS

# SHADOW ME

# ONE

I'm already awake when my alarm goes off, but I haven't opened my eyes yet. I'm too tired. My muscles are tight, still painfully sore from an intense training session two days ago, and my body feels heavy. Dead.

My brain hurts.

The alarm is shrill and persistent. I ignore it. I stretch out the muscles in my neck and groan, quietly. The clock won't stop screeching. Someone pounds, hard, against the wall near my head, and I hear Adam's muffled voice shouting at me to shut off the alarm.

"Every morning," he shouts. "You do this every morning. I swear to God, Kenji, one of these days I'm going to come in there and destroy that thing."

"All right," I mumble, mostly to myself. "All right. Calm down."

"*Turn it off.*"

I take a deep, ragged breath. Slap blindly at the clock until it stops blaring. We finally got our own rooms on base, but I still can't seem to find peace. Or privacy. These walls are paper thin, and Adam hasn't changed a bit. Still moody. No sense of humor. Generally irritated. Sometimes I can't remember why we're friends.

With some effort, I drag myself up, into a sitting position. I rub at my eyes, making a mental list of all the things I have to do today, and then, in a sudden, horrible rush—

I remember what happened yesterday.

*Jesus.*

So much drama in one day I can hardly keep it all straight.

Apparently Juliette has a long-lost sister. Apparently Warner tortured Juliette's sister. Warner and Juliette broke up. Juliette ran off screaming. Warner had a panic attack. Warner's ex-girlfriend showed up. His ex-girlfriend *slapped* him. Juliette got drunk. No, wait—J got drunk *and* she shaved her head. And then I saw Juliette in her underwear—an image I'm still trying to erase from my mind—and then, as if all that wasn't enough to deal with, after dinner last night, I did something very, very stupid.

I drop my head in my hands and hate myself, remembering. A fresh wave of embarrassment hits me, hard, and I take another deep breath. Force myself to look up. To clear my thoughts.

Not everything is horrible.

I have my own room now—a small room—but my own room with a window and a view of industrial AC units. I have a desk. A bed. A basic closet. I still have to share a bathroom with some of the other guys, but I can't complain. A private room is a luxury I haven't had in a while. It's nice to have space at the end of the night to be alone with my thoughts. Somewhere to hang the happy face I force myself to wear even when I'm having a shitty day.

I'm grateful.

I'm exhausted, overworked, and stressed out, but I'm grateful.

I force myself to say it, out loud. *I'm grateful.* I take a few moments to feel it. Recognize it. I force myself to smile, to unclench the tightness in my face that would otherwise default too easily to anger. I whisper a quick thank-you to the unknown, to the air, to the lonely ghosts eavesdropping on my private conversations with no one. I have a roof over my head and clothes on my back and food waiting for me every morning. I have friends. A makeshift family. I'm lonely but I'm not alone. My body works, my brain works, I'm alive. It's a good life. I have to make a conscious effort to remember that. To choose to be happy every day. If I didn't, I think my own pain would've killed me a long time ago.

*I'm grateful.*

Someone knocks at my door—two sharp raps—and I jump to my feet, startled. The knock is unusually formal; most of us don't even bother with the courtesy.

I yank on a pair of sweatpants and, tentatively, open the door.

*Warner.*

My eyes widen as I look him up and down. I don't think he's ever shown up at my door before, and I can't decide what's weirder: the fact that he's here or the fact that he looks so normal. Well, normal for Warner. He looks exactly like he always does. Shiny. Polished. Eerily calm and pulled together for someone whose girlfriend dumped him the day before. You'd never know he was the same dude who, in the aftermath, I found lying on the floor having a panic attack.

"Uh, hey." I clear the sleep from my throat. "What's going on?"

"Did you just wake up?" he says, looking at me like I'm an insect.

"It's six in the morning. Everyone in this wing wakes up at six in the morning. You don't have to look so disappointed."

Warner peers past me, into my room, and for a moment, says nothing. Then, quietly: "Kishimoto, if I considered other people's mediocre standards a sufficient metric by which to measure my own accomplishments, I'd never have amounted to anything." He looks up, meets my eyes. "You should demand more of yourself. You're entirely capable."

"Are you—?" I blink, stunned. "I'm sorry, was that your idea of a compliment?"

He stares at me, his face impassive. "Get dressed."

I raise my eyebrows. "You taking me out to breakfast?"

"We have three more unexpected guests. They just arrived."

"*Oh.*" I take an unconscious step back. "Oh shit."

"Yes."

"More kids of the supreme commanders?"

Warner nods.

"Are they dangerous?" I ask.

Warner almost smiles, but he looks unhappy. "Would they be here if they weren't?"

"Right." I sigh. "Good point."

"Meet me downstairs in five minutes, and I'll fill you in."

"Five minutes?" My eyes widen. "Uh-uh, no way. I need to take a shower. I haven't even eaten breakfast—"

"If you'd been up at three, you would've had time for all that and more."

"Three in the morning?" I gape at him. "Are you out of your mind?"

And when he says, without a hint of irony—

"No more than usual"

—it's crystal clear to me that this dude is not okay.

I sigh, hard, and turn away, hating myself for always noticing this kind of thing, and hating myself even more for my constant need to follow up. I can't help it. Castle said it to me once when I was a kid: he told me I was unusually compassionate. I never thought about it like that—with words, with an explanation—until he'd said it to me. I always hated it about myself, that I couldn't be tougher. Hated that I cried so hard when I saw a dead bird for the first time. Or that I used to bring home all the stray animals I found until Castle finally told me I had to stop, that we didn't have the resources to keep them all. I was twelve. He made me let them go, and I cried for a week. I hated that I cried. Hated that I couldn't help it. Everyone thinks I'm not supposed to give a shit—that I shouldn't—but I do. I always do.

And I give a shit about this asshole, too.

So I take a tight breath and say, "Hey, man— Are you all right?"

"I'm fine." His response is fast. Cold.

I could let it go.

He's giving me an out. I should take it. I should take it and pretend I don't notice the strain in his jaw or the raw, red look around his eyes. I've got my own problems, my own burdens, my own pain and frustration, and besides, no one ever asks me about my day. No one ever follows up with me, no one ever bothers to peer beneath the surface of my smile. So why should I care?

I shouldn't.

*Leave it alone*, I tell myself.

I open my mouth to change the subject. I open my mouth to move on, and, instead, I hear myself say—

"C'mon, bro. We both know that's bullshit."

Warner looks away. A muscle jumps in his jaw.

"You had a hard day yesterday," I say. "It's all right to have a rough morning, too."

After a long pause, he says, "I've been up for a while."

I blow out a breath. It's nothing I wasn't expecting. "I'm sorry," I say. "I get it."

He looks up. Meets my eyes. "Do you?"

"Yeah. I do."

"I don't think you do, actually. In fact, I hope you don't. I wouldn't want you to know how I feel right now. I wouldn't wish that for you."

That hits me harder than I expect. For a moment I don't know what to say.

I decide to stare at the floor.

"Have you seen her yet?" I ask.

And then, so quietly I almost miss it—

"No."

Shit. This kid is breaking my heart.

"Don't feel sorry for me," he says, his eyes flashing as they meet mine.

"What? I don't— I'm not—"

"Get dressed," Warner says sharply. "I'll see you downstairs."

I blink, startled. "Right," I say. "Cool. Okay."

And then he's gone.

# TWO

I stand in the doorway for a minute, running my hands through my hair and trying to convince myself to move. I've developed a sudden headache. Somehow, I've become a magnet for pain. Other people's pain. My own pain. The thing is, I have no one to blame but myself. I ask the follow-up questions that land me here. I care too much. I make it my business when I shouldn't, and I only ever seem to get shit for it.

I shake my head and then—*wince*.

The only thing Warner and I seem to have in common is that we both like to blow off steam in the gym. I pushed too much weight the other day and didn't stretch afterward—and now I'm paying for it. I can hardly lift my arms.

I take a deep breath, arch my back. Stretch my neck. Try to work out the knots in my shoulder.

I hear someone whistle down the hall and I look up. Lily winks at me in an obvious, exaggerated way, and I roll my eyes. I'd really like to be flattered, because I'm not modest enough to deny that I have a nice body, but Lily could not give fewer shits about me. Instead, she does this—mocks me for walking around without a shirt on—nearly every morning. Her *and* Ian. Together. The two have been low-key dating for a couple of months now.

"Looking good, bro." Ian smiles. "Is that sweat or baby oil? You're so shiny."

I flip him off.

"Those purple boxers are really working for you, though," says Lily. "Nice choice. They suit your skin tone."

I shoot her an incredulous look. I might not be wearing a shirt, but I'm definitely—I glance down—wearing sweatpants. My underwear is nowhere in sight. "How could you *possibly* know the color of my boxers?"

"Photographic memory," she says, tapping her temple.

"Lil, that doesn't mean you have X-ray vision."

"You're wearing purple underwear?" Winston's voice— and a distinct whiff of coffee—carries down the hall. "That's inspired."

"All right, fuck off, all of you."

"Hey— Whoa— I thought you weren't allowed to use foul language." Winston comes into view, his boots heavy on the concrete floor. He's fighting back a laugh when he says, "I thought you and Castle had an agreement."

"That's not true," I say, pointing at him. "Castle and I agreed I could say *shit* as much as I wanted."

Winston raises his eyebrows.

"Anyway," I mutter, "Castle isn't here right now, is he? So I stand by my original statement. Fuck off, all of you."

Winston laughs, Ian shakes his head, and Lily pretends to look offended, when—

"I most definitely *am* here right now, and I heard that," Castle calls from his office.

I cringe.

I used to swear profusely as a teenager—much worse than I do now—and it really used to upset Castle. He said he worried I'd never find a way to articulate my emotions without anger. He wanted me to slow down when I spoke, to use specific words to describe how I was feeling instead of angrily shouting obscenities. He seemed so worried about it that I agreed to tone down my language. But I made that promise four years ago, and as much as I love Castle, I often regret it.

"Kenji?" Castle again. I know he's waiting for an apology.

I peer down the hall and spot his open door. We're all squeezed up against each other, even with the new accommodations. Warner basically had to reinvent this floor, and it took a lot of work and sacrifice, so, again, I'm not complaining.

But still.

It's hard not to be annoyed by the overwhelming lack of privacy.

"My bad," I shout back.

I can actually hear Castle sigh, even from across the hall.

"A touching display of remorse," Winston says.

"All right, show's over." I wave them all away. "I have to shower."

"Yeah you do," Ian says, raising an eyebrow.

I shake my head, exhausted. "I can't believe I put up with you assholes."

Ian laughs. "You know I'm messing with you, right?" When I don't respond he says, "Seriously—you look good.

We should hit the gym later. I need someone to spot me."

I nod, only a little mollified, and mumble a goodbye. I head back into my room to grab my shower caddy, but Winston follows me in, leans against the doorframe. It's just then that I notice he's holding a paper to-go cup.

My eyes light up. "Is that coffee?"

Winston pulls away from the door, horrified. "It's *my* coffee."

"Hand it over."

"What? No."

I narrow my eyes at him.

"Why can't you get your own?" he says, pushing his glasses up the bridge of his nose. "This is only my second cup. You know it takes at least three before I'm even half awake."

"Yeah, well, I have to be downstairs in five minutes or Warner's going to murder me and I haven't had any breakfast yet and I'm already exhausted and I really—"

"Fine." Winston's face darkens as he hands it over. "You monster."

I take the cup. "I'm a goddamn *joy*."

Winston mutters something foul under his breath.

"Hey"—I take a sip of the coffee—"by the way— Did you, uh—?"

Winston's neck goes suddenly red. He averts his eyes. "No."

I hold up my free hand. "Hey—no pressure or anything. I was just wondering."

"I'm still waiting for the right time," he says.

"Cool. Of course. I'm just excited for you, that's all."

Winston looks up. Shoots me an uncertain smile.

Winston's been in love with Brendan for a long time, but I'm the only one who knows about it. Winston never thought Brendan would be interested, because as far as we knew, he'd only ever dated women, but a few months ago Brendan was linked, briefly, to this other dude from Point, and that was when Winston opened up to me about the whole thing. He asked me to keep it to myself, said he wanted to be the one to talk about it when it felt right, and he's been trying to build up the courage to say something to Brendan ever since. The problem is that Winston thinks he's a little old for Brendan, and he's worried that if Brendan turns him down it might ruin their friendship. So he's been waiting. For the right moment.

I clap him on the shoulder. "I'm happy for you, bro."

Winston lets out a breathy, nervous laugh that's unlike him. "Don't be too happy just yet," he says. And then he shakes his head as if to clear it. "Anyway—enjoy the coffee. I need to go get another one."

I raise the coffee cup in a gesture that says both *thank you* and *goodbye*, and as I turn away to gather my things for a quick shower, my smile slips. Somehow I can't help but be reminded, all the time, of my own solitude.

I kill the coffee in a couple of quick, deep pulls, and toss the cup. Quietly, I make my way to the shower, my movements mechanical as I turn on the water. Strip. Lather. Rinse. Whatever.

I'm frozen for a moment, watching the water pool in my upturned hands. I sigh, press my forehead to the cool, slick tile as the hot water pelts my back. I feel a measure of relief as my muscles begin to relax, the heat and steam releasing knots of tension under my skin. I try to focus on the luxury of this shower, on my gratitude for this miracle of hot water, but my less gracious thoughts keep circling me, pecking at my heart and mind like emotional vultures.

I'm so happy for my friends. I love them, even when they piss me off. I care about them. I want their joy. But it still hurts a little when it feels like, everywhere I look, everyone seems to have someone.

Everyone but me.

It's crazy how much I wish I didn't care. I wish, so much, all the time, that I didn't give a shit about this sort of thing—that I could be like Warner, a frozen, unforgiving island; or even like Adam, who's found his happiness in family, in his relationship with his brother—but I'm like neither. Instead, I'm a big, raw, bleeding heart, and I spend my days pretending not to notice that I want more. That I *need* more.

Maybe it sounds weird to say, but I know I could love the shit out of someone. I feel it, in my heart. This capacity to love. To be romantic and passionate. Like it's a superpower I have. A gift, even.

And I've got no one to share it with.

Everyone thinks I'm a joke.

I run my hands down my face, squeezing my eyes shut as I remember my interaction with Nazeera last night.

She came up to *me*, I try to remind myself.

I never approached her. I didn't even try to talk to her again, not after that day on the beach when she made it clear she wasn't even a little bit interested in me. Though it's not like I would've had a chance to talk to her after that, anyway; everything got crazy after that. J got shot and everyone was reeling, and then all that shit with Warner and Juliette went down, and now here we are.

But last night I was just minding my own business, still trying to figure out what to do about the fact that our supreme commander was slowly marinating in half a pint of Anderson's best whisky, when Nazeera came up to me. Out of the blue. It was right after dinner—hell, she wasn't even present at dinner—and she just showed up, like an apparition, cornering me as I was leaving the dining room. Literally backed me into a corner and asked me if it was true, that I had the power of invisibility.

She looked so mad. I was so confused. I didn't know how she knew and I didn't know why she cared, but there she was, right in front of me, demanding an answer, and I didn't see the harm in telling her the truth.

So I said yes, it was true. And she looked suddenly angrier.

"Why?" I said.

"Why what?" Her eyes flashed, big and wide and electric with feeling. She was wearing a leather hood, and the lights of a nearby chandelier glinted off the diamond piercing near her bottom lip. I couldn't stop staring at her mouth. Her lips

14

were slightly parted. Full. Soft.

I forced myself to look up. "What?"

She narrowed her eyes. "What are you talking about?"

"I thought— I'm sorry, what are we talking about?"

She turned away, but not before I saw the look of disbelief on her face. There might've been outrage, too. And then, lightning fast, she spun back around. "Are you just pretending to be dumb all the time? Or do you always talk like you're drunk?"

I froze. Pain and confusion swirled in my head. Pain from the insult, and confusion from—

Yeah, I had no idea what was happening.

"What?" I said again. "I don't talk like I'm drunk."

"You're looking at me like you're drunk."

Shit, she was pretty.

"I'm not drunk," I said. Stupidly. And then I shook my head and remembered to be angry—she'd just insulted me, after all—and I said, "Anyway, you're the one who came after me, remember? You started this conversation. And I don't know why you're so mad— Hell, I don't even know why you care. It's not my fault that I can be invisible. It just happened to me."

And then she shoved her hood back from her face and her hair shook out, dark and silky and heavy, and she said something I didn't hear because my brain was freaking out, like, should I tell her that I can see her hair? Does she know that I can see her hair? Did she mean for me to see her hair? Would she freak out, right now, if I told her that I could see

15

her hair? But then, also, just in case I wasn't supposed to be seeing her hair right now, I didn't want to tell her that I could see her hair because I was afraid she'd cover it up again, and, if I was being honest, I was really enjoying the view.

She snapped her fingers in my face.

I blinked. "What?" And then, realizing I'd overused that word tonight, I added a "Hmm?"

"You're not listening to me."

"I can see your hair," I said, and pointed.

She took a deep, irritated breath. She seemed impatient. "I don't always cover my hair, you know."

I shook my head. "No," I said dumbly. "I did not know that."

"I couldn't, even if I wanted to. It's illegal, remember?"

I frowned. "Then why have you been covering your hair? And why'd you give me such a hard time about it?"

She unhooked the hood from around her shoulders and crossed her arms. Her hair was long. Dark. Her eyes were deep. They were a light, honey color, bright against her brown skin. She was so beautiful it was scaring me.

"I know a lot of women who lost the right to dress like that under The Reestablishment. There was a huge Muslim population in Asia, did you know that?"

She doesn't wait for me to respond.

"I had to watch, quietly, as my own father sent down the decrees to have the women stripped. Soldiers paraded them into the streets and tore the clothing from their bodies.

Ripped the scarves from their heads and publicly shamed them. It was violent and inhumane, and I was forced to bear witness. I was eleven years old," she whispered. "I hated it. I hated my father for doing it. For making me watch. So I try to honor those women, when I can. For me, it's a symbol of resistance."

"Huh."

Nazeera sighed. She looked frustrated, but then—she laughed. It wasn't a funny laugh, it was more like a sound of disbelief, but I thought of it as progress. "I just told you something really important to me," she said, "and all you can say is *huh*?"

I thought about it. And then, carefully:

"No?"

And somehow, for some unknowable reason, she smiled. She rolled her eyes as she did it, but her face lit up and she looked suddenly younger—sweeter—and I couldn't stop staring at her. I didn't know what I'd done to earn that look on her face. I'd probably done nothing to earn it. She was probably laughing at me.

I didn't care.

"I, uh, think that's really cool," I said, remembering to say something. To acknowledge the importance of what she'd shared with me.

"You think *what's* cool?" She raised an eyebrow.

"You know." I nodded in the direction of her head. "Your whole—thing. That story. You know."

That's when she laughed for real. Out loud. She bit her

lip to cut the sound and she shook her head as she said, softly, "You're not messing with me, are you? You're just really bad at this."

I blinked at her. I didn't think I understood the question.

"You're terrible at talking to me," she said. "I make you nervous."

I blanched. "I didn't— I mean, I wouldn't say that y—"

"I think maybe I've been a little hard on you," she said, and sighed. She looked away. Bit her lip again. "I thought— that first night I met you—I thought you were trying to be an asshole. You know?" She met my eyes. "Like, I thought you were playing mind games with me. Being hot and cold on purpose. Insulting me one minute, asking me out the next."

"What?" My eyes widened. "I'd never do that."

"Yeah," she said softly. "I think I'm realizing that. Most of the guys I've known have been manipulative, condescending jackasses—my brother included—so I guess I wasn't expecting you to be so . . . honest."

"Oh." I frowned. I wasn't sure if she meant that to be a compliment. "Thank you?"

She laughed again. "I think we should start over," she said, and held out her hand as if to shake mine. "I'm Nazeera. It's nice to meet you."

Tentatively, I took her hand. Held my breath. Her skin was smooth, soft against my calloused palm. "Hi," I said. "I'm Kenji."

She smiled. It was a happy, genuine smile. I had a feeling

that smile was going to kill me. In fact, I was pretty sure this whole situation was going to kill me.

"That's a great name," she said, dropping my hand. "You're Japanese, right?"

I nodded.

"Do you speak?"

I shook my head.

"Yeah. It's tough. Beautiful but tough. I studied Japanese for a few years," she explained, "but it's a difficult language to master. I still have only a rudimentary grasp on it. I actually lived in Japan—well, what used to be Japan—for a month. I did a pretty extensive tour of the re-mapped Asian continent, actually."

And then I think she asked me another question, but I'd gone suddenly deaf. I'd lost my head. She was talking to me about the country my parents were born in—a place that really means something to me—and I couldn't even concentrate. She touched her mouth a lot. Ran her finger along the edge of her bottom lip a lot. She had a habit of tapping, often, at the diamond piercing there, and I'm not sure she was even aware she was doing it. But it was almost like she was telling me—directing me—to look at her mouth. I couldn't help it. I was thinking about kissing her. I was thinking about a lot of things. Pinning her to the wall. Undressing her slowly. Running my hands down her naked body.

And then, suddenly—

Taking a cold shower.

All at once, her smile faded. Her voice was soft, a little

concerned when she said, "Hey, are you okay?"

Not okay.

She was too close. She was too close and my body was definitely overreacting to her and I didn't know how to cool off. Shut down.

"Kenji?"

And then she touched my arm. She touched my arm and then seemed surprised she'd done it, just stared at her hand on my bicep and I forced myself to remain still, forced myself not to move a muscle as her fingertips grazed my skin and a wave of pleasure flooded my body so fast I felt suddenly drunk.

She dropped her hand and looked away. Looked back at me.

She looked confused.

"Shit," I said softly. "I think I might be in love with you."

And then, with a seismic jolt of terror, sense was knocked sideways into my head. I bolted upright in my own skin. I thought I might die. I thought I might actually *die* of embarrassment. I wanted to. I wanted to melt into the Earth. Evaporate. Disappear.

Jesus, I nearly did.

I couldn't believe I'd said the words out loud. I couldn't believe I'd been betrayed by my own goddamn mouth like that.

Nazeera stared at me, stunned and still processing, and somehow—through nothing short of a miracle—I managed to recover.

I laughed.

*Laughed.* And then I said, with perfect nonchalance, "I'm joking, obviously. I think I'm just exhausted. Anyway, good night."

I managed to walk, not run, back to my room, and was able to hold on to what was left of my dignity. I hope.

Then again, who the hell knows.

I'm going to have to see her again, probably very soon, and I'm sure she'll let me know if I should make plans to fly directly into the sun.

*Shit.*

I turn off the water and stand there, still sopping wet. And then, because I hate myself, I take a deep breath and turn on the cold water for ten, painful seconds.

It does the trick. Clears my head. Cools my heart.

I trip getting out of the shower.

I drag myself across the hall, forcing my legs to bend, but I'm still moving like I'm injured. I glance at the clock on the wall and swear under my breath. I'm late. Warner is going to kill me. I really need to spend an hour stretching—my muscles are still way too tight, even after a hot shower—but I have no time. And then, with a grimace, I realize that Warner was right. A couple extra hours to myself this morning would've done me a lot of good.

I sigh, heavily, and move toward my room.

I'm wearing my sweatpants, but I have only a towel draped around my neck because I'm in too much pain to pull a shirt over my head. I figure maybe I can steal one of Winston's button-downs—something I can slip on and off more easily than one of my own sweaters—when I hear someone's voice. I glance back, distracted, and in those two seconds I lose sight of where I'm going and slam into someone.

*Someone.*

Words fly out of my head. Just like that.

Gone.

I'm an idiot.

"You're *wet*," Nazeera says, wrinkling her nose as she jumps backward. "Why are you—"

And then I watch her, watch as she looks down. Looks up. Scans my body, slowly. I watch her look away and clear her throat, and suddenly she can't meet my eyes.

Hope blooms in my chest. Unlocks my tongue.

"Hey," I say.

"Hey." She nods. Crosses her arms. "Good morning."

"You need something?"

"Me? No."

I fight back a smile. It's strange to see her flustered. "Then what are you doing here?"

She's squinting at something behind me. "Do you—um, do you always walk around without a shirt on?"

I raise my eyebrows. "Up here? Yeah. Pretty much all the time."

She nods again. "I'll remember that." When I say nothing, she finally meets my eyes. "I was looking for Castle," she says quietly.

22

"His office is down that way"—I gesture with my head—"but he's probably made his way downstairs by now."

"Oh," she says. "Thanks."

She's still looking at me. She's still looking at me and it's causing my chest to constrict. I take a step forward almost without realizing it. Wondering, just wondering. I don't know what she's thinking. I don't know if I managed to screw everything up last night. But for some reason, right now—

She's staring at my mouth.

Her eyes move up, meet mine, and then she's staring at my mouth again. I wonder if she knows she's doing it. I wonder if she has any idea what she's doing to me. My lungs feel too small. My heart feels both fast and absurdly heavy.

When Nazeera meets my eyes again she takes a sudden, sharp breath. We're so close I can feel her exhalation against my bare chest and I'm overwhelmed by a disorienting need to kiss her. I want to pull her into my arms and kiss her, and for a moment I actually think she might let me. Just the thought of it sends a thrill up my spine, a dizzying feeling that inspires my mind to jump too far, too fast. I can picture it with terrifying clarity—the fantasy of having her in my arms, her eyes dark and heavy with desire. I can imagine her under me, her fingers digging into my shoulder blades as she screams—

*Jesus Christ.*

I force myself to turn away. I almost slap myself in the face.

I'm not this guy. I'm not some fifteen-year-old boy who can't keep his pants on. I'm not.

"I, uh, I have to get dressed," I say, and even I can hear the unsteadiness in my voice. "I'll see you downstairs."

But then Nazeera's hand is on my arm again, and my body stiffens, like I'm trying to contain something beyond myself. It's wild. Desire like I've never known it before. I try to remind myself that that's all this is, that it's like what J said—I don't even know this girl. I'm just going through something. I don't know what, or why, but I'm just, like, clearly infatuated. I don't even know her.

*This isn't real.*

"Hey," she says.

I hold still.

"Yeah?" I'm hardly breathing. I have to force myself to turn back an inch, meet her eyes.

"I wanted to tell you something. Last night. But I didn't have the chance."

"Oh." I frown. "Okay." There's something in her voice that sounds almost like fear—and it clears my head in an instant. "Tell me."

"Not here," she says. "Not now."

And I'm suddenly worried. "Is something wrong? Are you okay?"

"Oh—no— I mean, yeah— I'm fine. It's just—" She hesitates. Offers me a half smile and a shrug. "I just wanted to tell you something. It's nothing important." She looks away, bites her lip. She bites that bottom lip a lot, I notice. "Well, it's important to me, I guess."

"Nazeera," I say, enjoying the sound of her name in my mouth.

She looks up.

"You're freaking me out a little. Are you sure you can't tell me right now?"

She nods. Shoots me a tight smile. "No need to freak out, I promise. It's really not a big deal. Maybe we can talk later tonight?"

My heart constricts again. "Sure."

She nods once more. We say goodbye.

But when I glance back, not a second after I've started walking away, she's already gone.

Disappeared.

# THREE

Warner is definitely pissed.

I'm super late, and Warner is waiting for me, perched carefully on a stiff chair in a conference room downstairs, staring at a wall.

I managed to snag a muffin on my way down, and I wipe quickly at my face, hoping I haven't left evidence around my mouth. I don't know how Warner feels about muffins, but I'm guessing he's not a fan.

"Hey," I say, and I sound out of breath. "What'd I miss?"

"This is my fault," he says, waving a hand around the room. He doesn't even look at me.

"I mean, I already *know* it's your fault," I say quickly, "but, like, just to be clear—what are we talking about?"

"This," he says. Finally, he looks at me. "This situation."

I wait.

"It's my fault," he says, pausing dramatically, "for thinking I could depend on you."

I make an effort not to roll my eyes. "All right, all right, calm down. I'm here now."

"You're thirty minutes late."

"Bro."

Warner looks suddenly tired. "The children of the

supreme commanders of Africa and South America are here. They're waiting in the adjacent room."

"Yeah?" I raise an eyebrow. "So what's the deal? What do you need from me?"

"I need you to be present," he says sharply. "I'm not sure I know exactly why they're here, but all rational thought points to impending war. It's my suspicion that they're here to spy on us and send word back to their parents. They've sent their children to affect an air of camaraderie. A feeling of nostalgia. Maybe they think they can appeal to our new, young commander with other young faces. In any case, I think it's important for us to show a strong, united front."

"So no J, then, huh?"

Warner looks up. He seems stunned, and for a second I see something like pain in his eyes. I blink and he's a statue again. "No," he says. "I still haven't seen her. And it's more important than ever that they don't know that." He takes a breath. "Where's Castle? He needs to be here, too."

I shrug. "I thought he was already down here."

"I saw him a moment ago. I'll collect him."

I drop down into a chair. "Cool."

Warner walks to the door and then hesitates. Slowly, he turns to face me. "You're having trouble again."

I look up, surprised. "What?"

"In love. You're having trouble in your love life. Is that why you were late?"

I feel the blood drain from my face. "How the hell would you know something like that?"

"You reek of it." He nods at me, my body. "You're practically emanating lovelorn agony."

I stare at him, stunned. I don't even know if it's worth denying.

"It's Nazeera, isn't it?" Warner says. His eyes are clear, free of judgment.

I force myself to nod.

"Does she return your affections?"

I shoot him a belligerent look. "How the hell am I supposed to know?"

Warner smiles. It's the first real emotion he's shown all morning. "I suspected she might eviscerate you," he says. "But I admit I thought she would use a knife."

I force out a humorless: "Ha."

"Be careful, Kishimoto. I find it necessary to remind you that she was raised to be lethal. I wouldn't cross her."

"Great," I mutter, dropping my head in my hands. "I feel so good about this. Thanks for the pep talk."

"You should also know that there's something she's hiding."

My head snaps up. "What do you mean?"

"I don't know, exactly. I only know she's hiding something. I don't yet know what it is. But I would advise you to tread cautiously."

I feel suddenly ill, my forehead pinched with panic. I wonder about her cryptic message earlier. What it was she wanted to say to me last night. What she still might say to me—tonight.

And then I realize—

"Wait a second." I frown. "Did you just give me dating advice?"

Warner tilts his head. A flicker of a smile again. "I'm merely returning the favor."

I laugh, surprised. "Thanks, man. I appreciate that."

He nods.

And then, with an elegant pivot, he opens the door and closes it behind him. The dude moves like a prince. He's always dressed like a prince. Shiny boots and fitted suits and shit.

I sigh, irrationally irritated.

Am I jealous? Damn, maybe I'm jealous.

Warner always seems so pulled together. He's always cold and cool. Always has a line, a comeback. A clear head. I bet he's never struggled like I have with a girl. Never had to work so hard t—

Wow.

I'm an idiot.

I don't know how I managed to forget that his girlfriend literally just broke up with him. *I was there.* I saw the fallout. Dude had a panic attack all over the floor. He was *crying.*

I sigh, hard, and run both hands through my hair.

I know it should make me feel better, but it only makes me feel worse to realize that Warner is just as prone to relationship failure as I am. It makes me think I don't stand a chance with Nazeera.

Ugh, I hate everything.

I wait a couple of minutes for Warner and Castle to return, and while I'm waiting, I tug another muffin out of my pocket. I stress-eat it, ripping off huge chunks and blindly shoving them in my mouth.

When Castle walks through the door I'm nearly choking on muffin crumbs, but I wheeze through a quick hello. Castle frowns, clearly disapproving of my general state, and I pretend not to notice. I wave and try to swallow the last of the muffin. My eyes are tearing a little.

Warner steps inside, closes the door behind them. "Why do you insist on eating like an animal?" he snaps at me.

I frown, begin to speak, and he cuts me off with one hand.

"Don't you *dare* speak to me with your mouth full."

I swallow too quickly and nearly choke, but I force the rest of the muffin down. I clear my throat before saying, "You know what? I'm tired of this shit. You always make fun of the way I eat, and it's not fair."

Warner tries to speak and I cut him off.

"No," I say. "I don't eat like an animal. I just happen to be *hungry*. And maybe you should spend a few years starving to death before you think about making fun of the way I eat, okay asshole?"

It's startling, how quickly it happens, but something changes in Warner's face. Not the tightness in his jaw or the furrow in his brow. But for a moment, the light goes out of his eyes.

He turns almost exactly forty-five degrees away from

me. And his voice is solemn when he says, "They're waiting for us in the next room."

"I accept your apology," I say.

Warner looks back at me. Looks away.

Castle and I follow him out of the room.

Okay, maybe I missed something, but these new kids don't seem that scary. There's a set of twins—a boy and a girl—who speak to each other very quickly in Spanish, and a tall black guy with a British accent. Haider and Nazeera and Lena are conspicuously absent, but everyone is being polite and pretending not to notice. They're all pretty nice, actually. Especially Stephan, the son of the supreme commander of Africa. He seems cool; I'm getting fewer serial-killer vibes from him than I have from the other kids. But he's wearing a bracelet on his left hand, something silver set with thick, heavy red stones that look like rubies, and I can't stop feeling like I've seen something like it before. I keep staring, trying to figure out why it feels familiar, when, all of a sudden—

Juliette shows up.

At least, I think it's Juliette.

She looks like a different person.

She steps into the room wearing an outfit I've never seen her in, black from head to toe, and she looks good—beautiful, as always—but different. She seems harder. Angrier. I didn't think I'd like the short hair on her—last night it was a botched, haphazard job—but she must've cleaned it up this morning. The cut is a uniform crop throughout. A simple, sleek buzz cut.

She makes it work.

"Good morning," she says, and her voice is so hollow that, for a moment, I'm stunned. She manages to make those two words sound *mean*, and it's so unlike her that it scares me.

"Damn princess," I say softly. "Is that really you?"

She looks at me for only a second, but it feels more like she looks *through* me, and something about the cold, poisonous expression in her eyes breaks my heart like nothing else.

I don't know what happened to my friend.

And then, as if this shit couldn't get more dramatic, Lena busts through the door like a freaking debutante. She was probably waiting in the wings for the right time to make her entrance. To throw Juliette off her game.

It doesn't work.

I watch, as if through water, as Juliette meets Lena for the first time. Juliette is stiff and superior, and I'm proud of her for being strong—but I can't recognize her in the moment.

J isn't like this.

She's not cold like this.

I've seen her get angry—hell, I've seen her lose her mind—but she's never been cruel. She's not *mean*. And it's not that I think Lena deserves better, because I don't. I don't give a shit about Lena. But this—this display—is so out of character for Juliette that it must mean she's hurting even more than I thought. More than I could've imagined. Like the pain has disfigured her.

I would know. I *know* her.

Warner might murder me if he knew I felt this way, but the truth is, I know Juliette better than anyone. Better than he does.

The math is simple: J and I have been closer, longer.

She and I have been through more shit together. We've had more time to talk about real things together. She's my closest friend.

Castle has been there for me, too, but he's like a father to me, and I can't talk to him or anyone else the way I do with Juliette. She's different. She gets me. I give her a lot of crap for being emotional all the time, but I love how empathetic she is. I love how she feels things so deeply that sometimes even joy manages to wound her. It's who she is. She's all heart.

And this—this version of her I'm seeing right now?

It's bullshit.

I can't accept it because I know it's not real. Because I know it means something is wrong.

Suddenly, a swell of angry voices breaks through my reverie.

I look up just in time to realize Lena has said something nasty. Valentina, one of the twins, turns on her, and I force myself to pay closer attention as she says—

"I should've cut off your ears when I had the chance."

My eyebrows shoot up my forehead.

I step forward, confused, and glance around the room for a clue, but a strange, uncomfortable tension has reduced everyone to silence.

"Uh, I'm sorry," I say, clearing my throat. "Am I missing something?"

More silence.

It's Lena who finally volunteers an explanation, but I already know better than to trust her when she says, "Valentina likes to play pretend."

Nicolás, the other twin, rounds on her in an instant, furiously firing back in Spanish. Valentina pats her brother on the shoulder. "No," she says, "you know what? It's okay. Let her talk. Lena thinks I like to pretend"—she says a word in Spanish—"I won't be pretending"—more words in Spanish.

Stephan's mouth drops open in what appears to be shock, but Lena just rolls her eyes, so I have no idea what just happened.

I frown. It's a frustrating conversation to follow.

But when I glance over at Juliette I realize, with welcome relief, that I'm not the only one feeling this way; J doesn't understand what they're talking about, either. Neither does Castle. And just as I think that Warner must be confused, too, he starts talking to Valentina in fluent Spanish.

Suddenly my head is spinning.

"Damn, bro," I say. "You speak Spanish, too, huh? I'm going to have to get used to this."

"We all speak many languages," Nicolás says to me. He still seems a little irritated, but I'm grateful for the explanation. "We have to be able to communi—"

Juliette cuts him off angrily. "Listen, guys, I don't care about your personal dramas. I have a massive headache and a million things to do today, and I'd like to get started."

*Ha.*

Of course. Juliette has a hangover.

I bet she's never had a hangover. And if this weren't, like, a life or death situation, I'd think it was kind of hilarious.

Nicolás says something softly in response to her, and then drops his head in a mini-bow.

I cross my arms. I don't trust him.

"What?" Juliette stares at him, confused. "I don't know what that means."

Nicolás smiles at her. He says something else in Spanish—and by now it's obvious he's screwing with her—and I nearly kick the little shit in the face.

Warner gets to him before I do. He says something to Nicolás, something else I don't understand, but somehow this makes Juliette angrier.

What a weird morning.

I hear Nicolás say, "We are pleased to meet you," in English, and I'm officially so goddamn confused I think I should just see myself out.

Juliette says, "I take it you'll all be attending the symposium today?"

Another douche-bow from Nicolás. More words in Spanish.

"That's a yes," Warner translates.

That seems to piss her off. She spins around, turns to face him. "What other languages do you speak?" she says, her eyes flashing, and Warner goes so suddenly still my heart hurts for him.

This moment is too real.

Warner and Juliette are both so full of shit today. They're pretending to be so hard, so cool and collected, and then— *this*. Juliette says one thing to him and Warner turns into an idiot. He's staring at her, too dumb to speak, and she's flushed, looking all hot and bothered just because he's looking at her.

*Jesus.*

I wonder if Warner has any idea what he looks like right now, staring at Juliette like all the words were shoved right out of his head, and then, with a jolt, I wonder if that's what I looked like when I was talking to Nazeera.

An involuntary shudder runs through me.

Finally, Stephan puts Warner out of his misery. He clears his throat and says, "We were taught many languages from a very young age. It was critical that the commanders and their families all knew how to communicate with one another."

Juliette looks down, collects herself. When she turns to Stephan, her face has lost most of its flush, but she still looks a little blotchy.

"I thought The Reestablishment wanted to get rid of all the languages," Juliette says. "I thought you were working toward a single, universal language—"

"*Sí*, Madam Supreme," Valentina says. (I know the word *sí*. It means yes. I'm not a complete idiot.) "That's true," she says. "But first we had to be able to speak with each other, no?"

And then—

I don't know why, but something about Valentina's response breaks something open in Juliette. She looks almost like herself again. Her face loses its tension. Her eyes are wide—almost sad.

"Where are you from?" she says quietly, and her voice is so unguarded it gives me hope—hope that the real J is still in there, somewhere. "Before the world was remapped," she says, "what were the names of your countries?"

"We were born in Argentina," the twins say.

"My family is from Kenya," Stephan says.

"And you've visited each other?" Juliette turns, scans their faces. "You travel to each other's continents?"

They nod.

"Wow," she says. "That must be incredible."

"You must come visit us, too, Madam Supreme," Stephan says, smiling. "We'd love to have you stay with us. After all," he says, "you are one of us now."

And just like that, Juliette's smile is gone.

Her face closes off. Shutters shut. She reverts back to the cold shell of a person she was when she walked in, and her voice is severe when she says, "Warner, Castle, Kenji?"

I clear my throat. "Yeah?"

I hear Castle say, "Yes, Ms. Ferrars?"

I glance over at Warner, but he doesn't say a word. He only stares at her.

"If we're done here, I'd like to speak with the three of you alone, please."

I look from Warner to Castle, waiting for someone to say something, but no one does.

"Uh, yeah," I say quickly. "No, uh, no problem." I shoot Castle a look, like, *What the hell?* And he jumps in with a "Certainly."

Warner is still staring at her. He says nothing.

I almost slap him.

Juliette seems to agree with my line of thinking, because she stalks off, looking extremely pissed off as she goes, and I start following her out the door when I feel a hand on my shoulder. A heavy hand.

I look up directly into Warner's eyes, and, I'm not going to lie—it's a disorienting experience. That dude has some wild eyes. Pale, ice green. It's a little unnerving.

"Give me a minute with her," he says.

I nod. Take a step back. "Yeah, whatever you need."

And he's gone. I hear him call after her, and I stand there awkwardly, watching the open door and ignoring the other kids in the room. I cross my arms. Clear my throat.

"So it's true, then," Stephan says.

I turn, surprised. "What do you mean?"

"They really love each other." He nods toward the open door. "Those two."

"Yeah," I say, confused. "It's true."

"We've heard about it, of course," Nicolás says. "But it's interesting to witness in person."

"Interesting?" I raise an eyebrow. "Interesting how?"

"It's rather moving," Valentina says, and she sounds like she means it.

Castle walks up to me then. "It's been at least a minute," he says quietly.

"Right." I nod. "Well, we'll see you kids later," I say to the room. "If you guys haven't had breakfast yet, feel free to grab some muffins from the kitchen. They're good. I had two."

# FOUR

I nearly stumble trying to stop in place when we get out into the hall. Warner and Juliette haven't gone far, and they're standing close together, clearly having a heated, important conversation.

"We should get out of here," I say to Castle. "They need space to talk."

But Castle doesn't answer right away. He's staring at them with an intense look on his face, and for the first time in my life, I see him differently.

Like I don't know him.

After everything Warner told me yesterday—about how Castle always knew Juliette had a complicated history, knew she was a critical asset, knew she'd been adopted, knew that her biological parents had donated her to The Reestablishment and that he'd sent *me* on an undercover mission to collect her—I've felt a little strange. Not bad, exactly. Just strange. All this isn't enough of a revelation for me to lose faith in Castle entirely; he and I have been through too much for me to doubt his love.

But I feel off.

Unsettled.

I want to ask him why he kept all this from me. I want to

demand an explanation. But for some reason, I can't bring myself to do it. Not yet, anyway. I think maybe I'm afraid to hear the answers to my own questions. I worry about what they might reveal about *me*.

"Yes," Castle finally says, the sound of his voice refocusing my thoughts. "Perhaps we should give them the space they need."

I shoot him an uncertain look. "You don't think they're good together, huh?"

Castle turns to me, surprised. "On the contrary," he says. "I think they're lucky to have found each other in this hellish world. But if they want a chance at happiness, they'll have to continue to heal. Individually." He turns away again, studies their figures in the distance. "I worry, sometimes, about the secrets between them. I want them to do the hard work of sucking out the poison from their past."

"Gross."

Castle smiles. "Indeed." He wraps his arm around my shoulder. Squeezes. "My greatest wish for you," he says, "is for you to see yourself the way that I do: as a brilliant, handsome, compassionate young man who would do anything for the people he loves."

I pull back, surprised. "What made you say that?"

"It's just something I've been reminding myself to say out loud." He sighs. "I want you to understand that Nazeera is a very, very lucky girl to be the object of your affections. I wish you would realize that. She is accomplished and beautiful, yes, but you—"

41

"Wait. What?" I feel suddenly nauseous. "How did y—?"

"Oh," Castle says, his eyes wide. "Oh, was it a secret? I didn't realize it was a secret. My apologies."

I grumble something foul.

He laughs. "I have to say, if you're interested in keeping it to yourself, you might want to change your tactics."

"What do you mean?"

He shrugs. "You don't see yourself around her. Your feelings are obvious to everyone. From anywhere."

I drop my head into my hands with a groan.

And when I finally look up, ready to respond, I'm so distracted by the scene in front of me that I forget to speak.

Warner and Juliette are having a *moment*.

A pretty passionate moment, right here, in the hall. I realize, as I watch them, that I've never seen them kiss before. I'm frozen. A little stunned. And I know I should, like, look away—I mean, I know in my head that I should? That it's the decent thing to do? But I'm kind of fascinated.

They clearly have crazy chemistry.

Their relationship never made a lot of sense to me—I couldn't understand how someone like Warner could be an emotional partner to anyone, much less someone like Juliette: a girl who eats, sleeps, and breathes emotion. I rarely saw him emote *anything*. I worried that Juliette was giving him too much credit, that she put up with too much of his bullshit in exchange for—I don't even know what. A sociopath with an extensive coat collection?

Mostly, I worried that she wasn't getting the kind of love she deserved.

But now, suddenly—

Their relationship makes sense. Suddenly everything she's ever said to me about him makes sense. I still don't think I understand Warner, but it's obvious that something about her lights a fire in him. He looks alive when she's in his arms. Human like I've never seen him before.

Like he's in love.

And not only in love, but beyond salvation. When they break apart they both look a little crazy, but Warner looks especially unhinged. His body is shaking. And when she suddenly takes off running down the hall, I know this won't end well.

My heart aches. For both of them.

I watch as Warner slumps back, against the wall, sinking into the stone until his limbs give out. He collapses onto the floor.

"I'll talk to him," Castle says, and the devastated look on his face surprises me. "You go find Ms. Ferrars. She shouldn't be alone right now."

I take a tight breath. "Got it." And then: "Good luck."

He only nods.

I have to pound on Juliette's door a few times before she finally opens it. She cracks it open an inch, says, "Never mind," and then tries to slam it closed.

I catch the door with my boot.

"Never mind what?" I lean my shoulder into the door, and with a little shove, I manage to squeeze my way inside. "What's going on?"

She stalks across the room, as far away from me as she can get.

I don't understand this. I don't understand why she's treating me like this. And I open my mouth to say exactly that when she says—

"Never mind, I don't want to talk to any of you. Please go away. Or maybe you can all go to hell. I don't actually care."

I flinch. Her words land like physical blows. She's talking to me like I'm the enemy, and I can't believe it. "Are you—wait, are you serious right now?"

"Nazeera and I are leaving for the symposium in an hour," she snaps at me. She still won't look at me, though. "I have to get ready."

"What?" First of all, when the hell did she become best friends with Nazeera? And second of all: "What's happening, J? What's wrong with you?"

She spins around, her face a stunning caricature. She looks mutinous. *What's wrong with me?* Oh, like you don't know?"

The force of her anger sends me a step back. I remind myself that this girl could probably kill me with the twitch of her hand if she wanted to. "I mean, I heard about what happened with Warner, yeah, but I'm pretty sure I just saw you guys making out in the hallway, so I'm, uh, really confused—"

"He *lied* to me, Kenji. He lied to me this whole time. About so many things. And so did Castle. So did *you*—"

"Wait, what?" This time I grab her arm before she has a

chance to walk away again. "Wait—I didn't lie to you about shit. Don't mix me up in this mess. I had nothing to do with any of it. Hell, I still haven't figured out what to say to Castle. I can't believe he kept all of this from me."

Juliette goes suddenly still. Her eyes widen, bright with unshed tears. And then, finally, I understand. She thought I'd betrayed her, too.

"You weren't in on all this?" she whispers. "With Castle?"

"Uh-uh. No way." I take a step forward. "I had no clue about any of this insanity until Warner told me about it yesterday."

She stares at me, still uncertain.

And I can't help it; I roll my eyes.

"Well, how am I supposed to trust you?" she says, her voice breaking. "Everyone's been lying to me—"

"J," I say, "c'mon." I shake my head, hard. I can't believe I even have to say this. I can't believe she doubted me—that she didn't talk to me about this sooner. "You know me," I say to her. "You know I don't bullshit. That's not my style."

A single tear escapes down the side of her face and the sight of it is simultaneously heartbreaking and reassuring. This is the girl I know. The friend I love. She's all heart.

She whispers, "You promise?"

"Hey." I hold out my hand. "Come here, kid."

She still seems a little skeptical, but she takes the necessary steps forward and I reel her in, pulling her against my chest and squeezing tight. She's so tiny. Like a little bird with hollow bones. You'd never know she was technically invincible. That she could probably melt the skin off my face if she wanted to. I squeeze a little tighter, run a hand up and down her back in a comforting, familiar gesture, and I feel her finally relax. I feel the exact moment when the tension leaves her body, when she collapses fully against my chest. Her tears soak through my shirt, hot and unrelenting.

"You're going to be okay," I whisper. "I promise."

"Liar."

I smile. "Well, there's a fifty percent chance I'm right."

"Kenji?"

"Mm?"

"If I find out you're lying to me about any of this, I swear to God I will rip all the bones out of your body."

I almost choke on a sudden, surprised laugh. "Uh, yeah, okay."

"I'm serious."

"Uh-huh." I pat her head. So fuzzy.

"I will."

"I know, princess. I know."

We settle into a comfortable silence, the two of us still holding on, and I'm thinking about how important this relationship is to me—how important Juliette is to me—when she says, suddenly:

"Kenji?"

"Mm?"

"They're going to destroy Sector 45."

"Who is?"

"Everyone."

Shock straightens my spine. I pull back, confused. "Everyone who?"

"All the other supreme commanders," Juliette says. "Nazeera told me everything."

And then, suddenly, I get it.

Her new friendship with Nazeera.

This must be the secret Warner said she was hiding—Nazeera must be a traitor to The Reestablishment. It's either that, or she's lying to all of us.

The latter doesn't seem likely, though.

Maybe I'm being foolishly optimistic, but Nazeera practically said as much to me the other night with her whole speech about wearing a symbol of resistance and hating her dad and honoring the women he shamed.

Maybe Nazeera's big secret is that she's actually here to help us. Maybe there's nothing to be afraid of. Maybe the woman is just *perfect*.

I'm suddenly grinning like an idiot. "So Nazeera is one of the good guys, huh? She's on our team? Trying to help you out?"

"Oh my God, Kenji, please focus—"

"I'm just saying." I hold up my hands, take a step back. "The girl is fine as hell is all I'm saying."

Juliette is looking at me like I've lost my mind, but she laughs. She sniffs, gently, and brushes away a few forgotten tears.

"So." I nod, encouraging her to speak. "What's the deal?

The details? Who's coming? When? How? Et cetera?"

"I don't know," Juliette says, shaking her head. "Nazeera is still trying to figure it out. She thinks maybe in the next week or so? The kids are here to monitor me and send back information, but they're coming to the symposium, specifically, because the commanders want to know how the other sector leaders will react to seeing me. Nazeera says she thinks the information will help inform their next moves. I'm guessing we have maybe a matter of *days*."

My eyes go painfully wide. A matter of *days* was not what I was expecting to hear. I was hoping for months. Weeks, at the very least.

This is bad.

"Oh," I say. "Shit."

"Yeah." Juliette shoots me a beleaguered look. "But when they decide to obliterate Sector 45, their plan is to also take me prisoner. The Reestablishment wants to bring me back in, apparently. Whatever that means."

"Bring you back in?" I frown. "For what? More testing? Torture? What do they want to do with you?"

"I have no idea," Juliette says, shaking her head. "I have no clue who these people are. My sister is apparently still being tested and tortured somewhere. So I'm pretty sure they're not bringing me back for a big family reunion, you know?"

"Wow." I look away. Blow out a breath. "That is some next-level drama."

"Yeah."

"So—what are we going to do?" I say.

Juliette studies me for a second. Her eyes pull together. "I mean, I don't know, Kenji. They're coming to kill everyone in Sector 45. I really don't think I have a choice."

I raise my eyebrows. "What do you mean?"

"I mean, I'm pretty sure I'll have to kill them first."

# FIVE

I leave Juliette's room in a daze. It doesn't seem right that so much horrible shit should be, like, *allowed* to go down in such a short period of time. There should be a fail-safe in the universe somewhere, something that automatically shuts down in the event of extreme human stupidity. Maybe an emergency lever. A button, even.

This is *ridiculous*.

I sigh, feeling suddenly sick to my stomach.

I guess we'll have to wait to discuss all this tonight, after the symposium, which is going to be its own kind of shitshow. There doesn't seem to be a point to attending the symposium now, but Juliette said she didn't want to bail, not this late in the game, so we're all supposed to make nice and act like everything is normal. Six hundred sector leaders gathered in the same room and we're supposed to make nice and act like everything is normal. I don't get it. It's no secret to anyone that we, as a sector, have betrayed the entire establishment, so I don't understand why we're even bothering to pretend. But Castle says maintaining these pretenses means something to the system, so we have to follow through. Jumping ship now is basically like flipping off the rest of the continent. It'd be a declaration of war.

Honestly, the ridiculousness of this whole thing would almost be funny if I didn't think we were all probably going to die.

What a day.


I spot Sonya and Sara on my way back to my room and I nod a quick greeting, but Sara grabs my arm.

"Have you seen Castle?" she says.

"We've been trying to get ahold of him for an hour," says Sonya.

The urgency in their voices sends a sudden spike of fear through my body, and the viselike grip Sara's still got on my arm isn't helping. It's not like either of them to be so anxious; for as long as I've known them, these two have always been gentle and generally calm—through everything.

"What's wrong?" I say. "What's going on? Anything I can do to help?"

They shake their heads at the same time. "We need to talk to Castle."

"Last I saw him, he was downstairs, talking to Warner. Why don't you page him? He's always wearing his earpiece."

"We've tried," Sonya says. "Several times."

"Can you at least tell me what this is about? Just so I don't have a heart attack?"

Sara's eyes widen. "Have you been experiencing chest pains?"

"Have you been feeling unusually lethargic?" Sonya chimes in.

"Shortness of breath?" Sara again.

"What? No. Guys, stop—I meant that as a figure of speech. I'm not actually going to have a heart attack. I'm just—I'm worried."

Sonya ignores me. She rummages around in the messenger bag she carries around in case of emergencies and unearths a small medicine bottle. She and Sara are twins and our resident healers—and they're an interesting combination of gentle but extremely serious. They're doctors with the perfect bedside manner, and they never let any mention of pain, illness, or injury go ignored. Once, back at Point, I said casually that I was sick and tired of being underground all the time, and the two of them forced me into a bed and demanded I give them a list of my symptoms. When I was finally able to explain that I'd been joking—that "sick and tired" was just a thing people say sometimes—they didn't think it was funny. They were irritated with me for a week after that.

"Take this with you, as a precaution," Sonya says, and presses the blue, cylindrical bottle into my hand. "As you know, Sara and I have been working on this for a while, but this is the first time we feel like it might be ready for the field. That," she says, nodding at the bottle in my hand, "is one of the test batches, but we haven't had any trouble with it. Actually, we think it might be ready for production."

That gets my attention.

I stare in awe at the bottle in my hand. It's heavy. Glass. "No way," I say softly. "You did it?" I look up, look into their eyes.

They smile at exactly the same time.

These two have been working on creating healing pills for as long as I can remember. They wanted to give us something to take on the road—in the middle of battle—to keep us going if and/or when they're not around.

"Did James work on this at all?"

Sonya smiles wider. "He helped."

"Yeah?" I smile, too. "How's his training going? Everything okay?"

They nod. "We're about to go pick him up, actually," Sara says. "For his afternoon session. He's a fast study. He's growing into his powers nicely."

Almost without realizing it, I stand up a bit taller, puff my chest like a peacock. I don't know what right I have to feel proprietary about that kid, but I'm so proud of him.

I know he's got a big future ahead of him.

"All right, well"—I hold up the bottle—"thank you for this. I'm going to take it with me, because"—I shake the bottle—"this is amazing. But don't worry. Seriously. I'm not going to have a heart attack."

"Good," they both say.

I grin. "So you want me to tell Castle you're looking for him?"

They nod.

"And you're not going to tell me what the urgency is all about?"

Sara and Sonya exchange glances.

I raise an eyebrow.

Finally, Sara says—

"Do you remember when Juliette was shot?"

"She was shot three days ago, Sara." I offer her an incredulous look. "I'm not likely to forget."

Sonya jumps in and says, "Yes, but, the thing you don't know—the thing that no one but Warner and Castle know—is that something happened to Juliette when she was shot. Something we weren't able to heal."

"What?" I say sharply. "What do you mean?"

"There was some kind of poison in the bullets," Sara explains. "Something that was giving her hallucinations."

I stare, horrified.

"We've been studying the properties of the poison for days, trying to come up with an antidote," she says. "Instead, we discovered something . . . unexpected. Something even more important."

After a beat of silence, I can't take it anymore.

*"And?"* I say, gesturing with my hand that they should continue.

"We really want to tell you everything," Sonya says, "but we have to speak to Castle first. He needs to be the first to know." She hesitates. "I can only tell you that we think we've discovered something that directly corresponds with the tattoos on the dead body of Juliette's assailant."

"That guy Nazeera killed," I say, remembering. "She saved Juliette's life."

They nod.

Another spike of fear spears through me.

"All right," I say, trying to keep my voice light, steady. I

54

don't want to freak them out with my own worries. "Okay. I'll tell Castle to come find you right away. Will you be in the medical wing?"

They nod again.

And then, as I walk away, Sara calls after me.

I turn around.

"Tell him—" She hesitates again, and then seems to make a decision. "Tell him it's about Sector 241. Tell him we think it's a message. From Nouria."

"What?" I freeze in place, disbelieving. "That's impossible."

"Yes," Sara says. "We know."

I take the stairs.

I don't have time to wait for the elevator, and besides, my body is too full of nervous energy right now to stand still. I take the stairs two, three at a time, flying even as I keep a hand on the handrail to steady myself.

I didn't think this day could get crazier.

Nouria.

Shit.

I don't know how Castle will react to hearing her name. He hasn't heard a word from Nouria in years. Not since— well, not since the boys were murdered. Castle told me he gave Nouria space because he thought she needed time. He figured they'd find their way back to each other again after she recovered. But after the sectors were erected, it became near impossible to contact loved ones. The internet was one of the first things The Reestablishment took away, and without it the world became—in an instant—a bigger, scarier place. Everything was harder. Everyone felt helpless. I don't think anyone realized just how much we relied on the internet for literally everything until the lights went off. Computers and phones were taken away. Destroyed. Hackers were found and publicly hanged.

Borders were closed without clearance.

And then The Reestablishment tore families apart. On purpose. In the beginning they pretended they were doing it for the good of humanity. They called it a new form of integration. They said race relations were at their worst because we were all so isolated from one another, and that part of the problem was that people had built these extensive family units—The Reestablishment referred to big families as dynasties—and that these dynasties only reinforced homogeneity within homogenous communities. They said that the only way to fix this was to rip those dynasties apart. They ran algorithms that helped them manufacture diversity by rebuilding communities with specific ratios.

But it wasn't long before they stopped pretending to give a shit about diverse communities. Soon, small infractions alone would be enough to have you taken from your family. Show up late to work one day and sometimes they'd send you—or worse, someone you loved—across the planet. So far away you'd never be able to find your way back.

That's what happened to Brendan. He was torn from his family and sent here, to Sector 45, when he was fifteen.

Castle found him and took him in. Lily, too. She's from what used to be Haiti. They took her from her parents when she was only twelve. They put her in a group home with a ton of other displaced children. They were glorified orphanages.

I ran away from one of those orphanages when I was eight.

Sometimes I think that's why I care about James so much. I feel connected to him, in a way. When we were on base together Adam never told me that his little brother practically lived in one of those orphanages. It wasn't until that day when we were on the run—when James and I had to hide out together while Adam and Juliette tried to find a car—that I realized where we were. I took one glance around those grounds and I saw that place for what it was.

All those kids.

James was luckier than the other children—not only did he have a living relative, but he had a relative who lived close by, one who could afford to keep him in a private apartment. But when I asked James about his "school" and his "friends" and about Benny, the woman who was supposed to bring him his government-issue meals on a regular basis, I got all the answers I needed.

James got to sleep in his own bed at night, but he spent his days in an orphanage, with other orphaned children. Adam paid Benny a little extra to keep an eye on James, but ultimately, her loyalty was to a paycheck. At the end of the day, James was a ten-year-old kid living all alone.

Maybe all this is why I feel like I understand Adam. Why

I fight for him, even when he's a dick. He comes off as an angry, explosive guy—and sometimes he really is an asshole—but it must be hard to watch your kid brother live all alone on a compound for tortured, abandoned children. It slowly kills your soul to watch a ten-year-old kid sob and scream in the middle of the night because his nightmares keep getting worse, and no matter what you do, you can't seem to make it better.

I lived with Adam and James for months. I saw the cycle every night. And I watched, every night, as Adam tried to calm James down. How he'd rock his little brother in his arms until the sun came up. I think James is finally doing better, but sometimes I'm not sure Adam will ever recover from the blows he's been dealt. It's obvious he has PTSD. I don't think he even sleeps anymore. I think he's slowly losing his mind.

And sometimes I wonder—

If I had to live with that every day, I wonder if it would make me crazy, too. Because it's not the pain that's unendurable. It's the hopelessness. It's the hopelessness that makes you reckless.

I would know.

It only took two hours in the orphanage before I realized I couldn't trust adults anymore, and by the time Castle found me on the run—a nine-year-old kid trying to keep warm in a shopping cart on the side of the road—I was so disillusioned with the world I thought I'd never recover. It took a long time for Castle to earn my trust completely; in the beginning, I spent all my free time picking locked doors and sneaking through his things when I thought he wasn't looking. The day he found me, sitting in his closet inspecting the contents of an old photo album, I was so sure he would take a bat to my back I nearly ruined my pants. I was terrified, unconsciously flickering in and out of invisibility. But instead of yelling at me, he sat down next to me and asked me about my family; I'd only ever told him that they were dead. He wanted to know now if I'd tell him what happened. I shook my head repeatedly. I wasn't ready to talk. I didn't think I'd ever be ready to talk.

He didn't get angry.

He didn't even seem to mind that I'd ransacked his personal belongings. Instead, he picked up the photo album in my lap and told me about his own family.

It was the first time I'd ever seen him cry.

# SIX

When I finally find Castle, he's not alone. And he's not okay.

Nazeera, Haider, Warner, and Castle are leaving a conference room at the same time, and only the siblings look like they're not about to vomit.

I'm still breathing hard, having just raced down six flights of stairs, and I sound winded when I say, "What's going on?" I nod at Warner and Castle. "Why do you two look so freaked out?"

"Let's discuss it later," Castle says quietly. He won't look at me.

"I have to go," Warner says, and bolts. Down the hall and far, far away.

I watch him leave.

Castle is about to slip away, too, but I grab his arm. "Hey," I say, forcing him to meet my eyes. "The girls need to talk to you. It's critical."

"Yes," he says, and he sounds strained. "I just saw all their messages. I'm sure it can wait until after the symposium. I need a minute to—"

"It can't wait." I hold his gaze. "It's *critical*."

Finally, Castle seems to grasp the gravity of what I'm trying to relay. His shoulders stiffen. His eyes narrow.

"Nouria," I say.

And Castle looks so stunned I worry he might fall over.

"I wouldn't bring you a bullshit message, sir. Go. Now. They're waiting in the medical wing."

And then he's gone, too.

"Who's Nouria?"

I look up to see Haider studying me curiously.

"His cat," I say.

Nazeera fights back a smile. "Castle received an urgent message from his cat?"

"I didn't know he had a cat," Haider says, his brows furrowing. He has a slight accent, unlike Nazeera, but his English is flawless. "I haven't seen any animals on base. Are you allowed to keep animals as pets in Sector 45?"

"Nah. But don't worry, it's an invisible cat."

Nazeera tries and fails to force back a laugh. She coughs, hard. Haider looks at her, confused, and I watch for the moment he realizes I've been screwing with him. And then—

He glares at me. "*Hemar.*"

"Say what?"

"He just called you an ass," Nazeera explains.

"Wow. Nice."

"*Hatha shlon damaghsiz,*" Haider says to his sister. "Let's go."

"Okay—wait—*that* sounded like it might be a compliment."

"Nope." Nazeera smiles wider. "He just said you're an idiot."

"Cool. Well, I'm glad to be learning all these important words in Arabic."

Haider shakes his head, outraged. "This was not meant to be a lesson."

I stare at him for a moment, genuinely baffled. "Your brother has no sense of humor, huh?" I say to Nazeera.

"He's not good with subtlety," she says, still smiling at me. "You have to knock him over the head with a joke or he doesn't get it."

I place a hand over my heart. "Wow, I'm so sorry. That must be so difficult for you."

She laughs but quickly bites her lip to kill the sound. And she sounds serious when she says, "You have no idea."

Haider frowns. "What are you talking about?"

"You see what I mean?" she says.

I laugh, staring into her eyes for just a second too long. Haider shoots me a murderous look.

I take that as my cue to leave.

"All right, yeah," I say, and take a quick breath. "I better get going. Symposium starts in"—I glance at my watch; my eyes widen—"thirty minutes. Shit." I look up. "Bye."

This thing is a *scene*.

There are around six hundred commanders and regents—officers at the same level as Warner—in the audience, and the place is buzzing. People are still settling in, taking their seats, and Juliette is up at the podium. The group of us are standing behind her, onstage with her, and I'm not going to lie—it feels a little risky. We're perfect targets for any psycho who might show up with a gun. We've taken precautions of course—no one is supposed to be allowed in here with any kind of weapon—but that doesn't mean it can't happen. But we all agreed that standing united like this would send the strongest message. The girls remained back on base—we decided it would be best for them to stay safe long enough to save us if we get injured—and James and Adam are MIA. Castle said that Adam doesn't want to participate in anything even remotely hostile anymore. Not unless he has to.

I get it.

In my less charitable moments I might call him a coward, but I get it. I'd opt out, too, if I could. I just don't feel like I can.

There's still too much I'm willing to die for.

Anyway. Juliette is pretty much invincible, so as long as she keeps her Energy on, she should be fine. The rest of us are vulnerable—but at the first sign of danger we're supposed to scatter. We're too outnumbered to fight; our best chance of survival is to spread out, spread far.

That's the plan.

That's the whole goddamn plan.

We hardly even had time to talk about the plan, because everything has been so insane lately, but Castle gave us all a quick pep talk before J took the stage, and that was it. That was all we were going to get. A quick *good luck and I hope you don't die.*

I'm definitely nervous.

I shift my weight, feeling suddenly restless, as the crowd goes still. It's a sea of military faces, the iconic red/green/blue stripes of The Reestablishment emblazoned on every uniform. I know they're regular people—blood and guts and bones—but they look like machines. And they turn their heads up at the same time, eyes blinking in unison as Juliette begins to speak.

It's creepy as hell.

We always knew that no one outside of Sector 45 would willingly accept Juliette as their new supreme commander, but it's chilling to witness in person. They clearly have no respect for Juliette, and as she talks about her love for the people, for the hardworking men and women whose lives were stripped for parts, I can see them strain to contain their anger. There's a reason so many are still loyal to The Reestablishment—and the proof of it is right here, in this room. These people are paid better. They're given perks, privileges. I never would've believed it if I hadn't seen it with my own eyes, but once you see the things people are willing to do for an extra bowl of rice, you can't unsee it. The Reestablishment keeps their higher-ups happy. They don't have to mingle with the masses. They get to keep their finery and live in real homes on unregulated territory.

These men and women sneering at Juliette as she speaks—they don't want her version of the world. They don't want to lose their rank and the privileges that rank affords. Everything she's saying about the failures of The Reestablishment, about the need to start over and give the people back their homes, their families, their *voices*—

Her words are a threat to their livelihood.

So it's really no surprise at all to me when the crowd decides they've had enough. I feel their restlessness growing more wild as she speaks, and when someone suddenly stands up and screams at her—*makes fun of her*—I worry this won't end well. Juliette keeps cool, keeps talking even as more of them jump to their feet and shout. They're shaking their fists and demanding she be removed from the podium, demanding she be executed for treason, demanding she be imprisoned, at the very least, for speaking against The Reestablishment, but her voice can hardly be heard over the crowd.

And then she starts shouting.

This is bad. This is really, really bad, and my instincts are telling me to panic, that this will only end in bloodshed. I'm trying to look around and still keep my cool, but when Warner catches my eye I know, right away, that he gets it. We're both thinking the same thing:

Abort mission.

Get the hell out of here as soon as possible.

And then—

"This was an ambush. Tell your team to run. Now."

I spin around in an exaggerated motion, so freaked out I nearly lose my balance. I'm hearing Nazeera. I'm hearing *Nazeera*. I'm sure I'm hearing her voice. The problem is, I don't see her anywhere.

Am I dying? I must be dying.

"*Kenji*. Listen to me."

I freeze in place.

I can feel the warmth of her body edging up against mine. I can feel her mouth at my ear, the gentle whisper of her breath against my skin. Jesus. I know how this works. I *invented* this shit.

"You're invisible," I say, so quietly I hardly move my lips.

I feel the tickle of her hair against my neck as she leans closer, and I have to suppress the urge to shiver. It's so strange. So strange to be feeling so many emotions at once. Terror, fear, worry, want. It's confusing. And her hand is on my arm when she says, "I was hoping to explain later. But now you know. And now you have to run."

Shit.

I turn to Ian, who's standing to the left of me, and say, "It's time to bail, bro. Let's go."

Ian looks at me, his eyes widening for a fraction of a second, and then he grabs Lily's hand and shouts, "Run—RUN—"

The sound of a gunshot splits open a moment of silence.

It feels like slow motion. It feels like the world slows down, turns on its side, and swings back around. Somehow I think I can see the bullet as it moves, fast and strong, right at Juliette's head.

It hits its mark with a dull thud.

I'm hardly breathing. I'm beyond pretending I'm not terrified. Shit just got real, super fast, and I have no idea what's about to happen. I know I need to move, need to get the hell out of here before things get worse, but— I don't know why, but I can't convince my legs to work. Can't convince myself to look away.

No one can.

The crowd has gone deathly still in the aftermath. People are staring at Juliette like they didn't believe the rumors. Like they wanted to know if it was really true that this seventeen-year-old girl could murder the most intimidating despot this nation has ever known, and then stand in front of a crowd and peel a bullet off her forehead after an attempted assassination, looking for all the world like the experience was no more annoying than swatting a fly.

I suppose now they know that the rumors were true.

But Juliette looks suddenly more than annoyed. She looks both surprised and furious as she stares at the ruined bullet in the palm of her hand. From this vantage point it looks like a mutilated coin. And then, disgusted, she tosses it to the ground. The sound of the metal hitting stone is delicate. Elegant.

And then—

That's it. Everyone goes apeshit.

People lose their goddamn minds. The crowd is on its feet, roaring threats and obscenities, and they all pull weapons from their bodies and I'm thinking, *Where the hell did they get them from? How did so many of them get through? Who's our mole?*

More gunshots split the air.

I swear, loudly, and move to tackle Castle to the

ground—and then I hear it. I *hear* it before I see it. The surprised gasp. The heavy thud. The reverberations of the stage under my feet.

Brendan is on the ground.

Winston is sobbing. Desperately, I push through my teammates, falling to my knees to assess the wound. Brendan's been shot in the shoulder. Relief sags my body. He'll be okay.

I toss the glass pill bottle at Winston and tell him to force a few down Brendan's throat, tell him to apply pressure to the wound and remind him that Brendan's going to be okay, that we just need to get him to Sonya and Sara—and then I remember.

*I remember.*

I know this girl.

I look up, panicked, and scream, "Juliette, DON'T—"

But she's already lost control.

# SEVEN

She's screaming.

*She's just screaming words*, I think. They're just *words*. But she's screaming, screaming at the top of her lungs, with an agony that seems almost an exaggeration, and it's causing devastation I never knew possible. It's like she just—imploded.

It doesn't seem real.

I mean, I knew Juliette was strong—and I knew we hadn't discovered the depth of her powers—but I never imagined she'd be capable of this.

Of this:

The ceiling is splitting open. Seismic currents are thundering up the walls, across the floors, chattering my teeth. The ground is rumbling under my feet. People are frozen in place even as they shake, the room vibrating around them. The chandeliers swing too fast and the lights flicker ominously. And then, with one last vibration, three of the massive chandeliers rip free from the ceiling and shatter as they hit the floor.

Crystal flies everywhere. The room loses half its light and suddenly, it's hard to see exactly what's happening. I look at Juliette and see her staring, slack-jawed, frozen at the sight of the devastation, and I realize she must've stopped screamed a moment ago. She can't stop this. She already put the energy into the world and now—

It has to go somewhere.

The shudders ripple with renewed fervor across the floorboards, ripping new cracks in walls and seats and *people*.

I don't actually believe it until I see the blood. It seems fake, for a second, all the limp bodies in seats with their chests butterflied open. It seems staged—like a bad joke, like a bad theater production. But when the blood arrives, heavy and viscous, seeping through clothes and upholstery, dripping down frozen hands, I know we'll never recover from this.

Juliette just murdered six hundred people at once.

There's no recovering from this.

# EIGHT

I shove my way through the quiet, stunned, still-breathing bodies of my friends. I hear Winston's soft, insistent whimpers and Brendan's steady, reassuring response that the wound isn't as bad as it looks, that he's going to be okay, that he's been through worse than this and survived it—

And I know my priority right now needs to be Juliette.

When I reach her I pull her into my arms, and her cold, unresponsive body reminds me of the time I found her standing over Anderson, a gun aimed at his chest. She was so terrified—*so surprised*—by what she'd done that she could hardly speak. She looked like she'd disappeared into herself somewhere—like she'd found a small room in her brain and had locked herself inside. It took a minute to coax her back out again.

She hadn't even killed anyone that time.

I try to warm some sense into her again, begging her now to return to herself, to hurry back to her mind, to the present moment.

"I know shit is crazy right now, but I need you to snap out of this, J. Wake up. Get out of your head. We have to get out of here."

She doesn't blink.

"Princess, please," I say, shaking her a little. "We have to go—*now*—"

And when she still doesn't move, I figure I have no choice but to move her myself. I start hauling her backward. Her limp body is heavier than I expect, and she makes a small, wheezing sound that's almost like a sob. Fear sparks in my nerves. I nod at Castle and the others to go, to move on without me, but when I glance around, looking for Warner, I realize I can't find him anywhere.

What happens next knocks the wind from my lungs.

The room tilts. My vision blackens, clears, and then darkens only at the edges in a dizzying moment that lasts hardly a second. I feel off-center. I stumble.

And then, all at once—

Juliette is gone.

Not figuratively. She's literally gone. Disappeared. One second she's in my arms, and the next, I'm grasping at air. I blink fast, convinced I'm losing my mind, but when I look around the room I see the audience members begin to stir. Their shirts are torn and their faces are scratched, but no one appears to be dead. Instead, they begin to stand, confused, and as soon as they start shuffling around, someone shoves me, hard. I look up to see Ian swearing at me, telling me to get moving while we still have a chance, and I try to push back, try to tell him that we lost Juliette—that I haven't seen Warner—and he doesn't hear me, he just forces me forward, offstage, and when I hear the murmur of the crowd grow into a roar, I know I have no choice.

I have to go.

# REVEAL
# ME

# ONE

I've lost my appetite.

I don't think I've ever lost my appetite.

But I'm staring at a perfectly good piece of cake right now, and for some reason, I can't eat it. I feel queasy.

I keep tapping the cake with the tines of my fork, each time a little harder, and now it's half-collapsed and the frosting is scarred. Mutilated. I never meant to disfigure an innocent piece of cake—it's downright criminal to waste food, especially cake—but there's something soothing about the repetitive motion and the soft, gentle resistance of the vanilla sponge.

Slowly, I drag my free hand down my face.

I've had worse days. Greater losses. Shittier nights. But somehow this feels like a new kind of hell.

Tension gathers in my shoulders, knotting together to generate dull, throbbing pain that branches across my back. I try to breathe it out, try to stretch the stress out of my muscles, but nothing helps. I don't know how long I've been sitting here, hunched over an unfinished slice of cake. Hours, maybe.

I take a glance around the half-empty dining hall. Room? Tent?

Definitely a tent.

I squint up at the long, whitewashed wooden beams supporting the ceiling. Maybe tent-adjacent. There's a cream-colored canvas shrouding everything on the outside, but it's obvious from the interior that this is a solid, freestanding building. I don't know why they bother with the tents. I hope they serve some kind of practical purpose, because otherwise it seems dumb. Everything else is pretty spare. The tables are pieced together with unfinished slabs of wood made smooth by time. The chairs are simple. More wood. Very basic. Nice, though; everything is nice. This place feels newer, cleaner, and brighter than anything we had at Omega Point. It's like a fancy campsite.

*The Sanctuary.*

I stab at the cake again. It's late—long past midnight—and my reasons for being here are growing more tenuous by the minute. Nearly everyone is bailing, chairs scraping, feet shuffling, doors opening and closing. Warner and Juliette (Ella? Still feels weird) are here somewhere, but that's probably because she's trying to force-feed him his own birthday cake. Or maybe he's eating it voluntarily. Whatever. When I'm feeling really sorry for myself, I hate him more than usual.

I squeeze my eyes shut. I'm so goddamn tired.

I know I should leave, get some sleep, but I can't make myself abandon the warm glow of this room for the cold loneliness of my tent. It's so bright in here. It's obvious that Nouria—Castle's daughter and the head of this resistance—is really into light. It's her specialty. Her super-power. But it's also everywhere. String lights strung across the ceiling. Lanterns lining the walls and doorways. There's a massive stone fireplace against one wall, but it's full of warm light, not fire. It feels cozy.

Plus, it smells like cake in here.

For years all I ever did was complain about having to share my privacy with people, but now that I've got my own place—a little stand-alone home entirely for myself—I don't want it. I miss the common areas at Omega Point and Sector 45. I liked seeing friends when I opened my door. I liked hearing their stupid, inconsiderate voices when I was trying to fall asleep.

So.

I'm still here.

Not yet ready to be alone.

Instead, I've been sitting here all night watching people pair off and disappear. Lily and Ian. Brendan and Winston. Sonya and Sara. Nouria and her wife, Sam. Castle trailing behind.

Everyone smiling.

They seem hopeful. Relieved. Celebrating survival and the rare moments of beauty in the bloodshed. Me, on the other hand, I want to scream.

I drop my fork, digging the heels of my hands into my eyes. My frustration has been building for hours now, and it's finally beginning to peak. I feel it, feel it closing its hands around my neck.

*Anger.*

Why am I the only one who's scared right now? Why am I the only one with this pit of nervousness in my gut? Why am I the only one asking the same question over and over and over again:

*Where the fuck are Adam and James?*

When we finally got to the Sanctuary, we were greeted by fanfare and joy and enthusiasm. Everyone was acting like this was a big family reunion, like there was hope for the future, like we were all going to be okay—

No one seemed to care that Adam and James were missing.

I was the only one doing a head count. I was the only one looking around the room, searching the eyes of unfamiliar faces, peering around corners and asking questions. I was the only one, apparently, who didn't think it was okay to be missing two of my teammates.

"He didn't want to come, man. You already know that."

This.

This was the bullshit explanation Ian tried to feed me earlier.

"Kent said he wasn't leaving anymore," Ian said. "He literally told us to make our plans without him, and you were sitting right there when he said it." Ian narrowed his eyes at me. "Don't lie to yourself about this. Adam wanted to stay behind with James and try for immunity. You heard him. Leave it alone."

But I couldn't.

I kept insisting that the situation felt wrong. The way it all went down—it felt wrong. *Something isn't right*, I kept saying, and Castle kept telling me, gently—like he was talking to a crazy person—that Adam is James's guardian, that it's not my business, that it doesn't matter how much I love James, I don't get to choose what happens to him.

The thing no one seems to remember is that Adam pitched that dumbass idea about staying behind and asking for immunity *before* we knew Anderson was still alive. *Before* we heard Delalieu say that Anderson had made secret plans for Adam and James. This was *before* Anderson showed up and murdered Delalieu and we all got thrown in an asylum.

Something is wrong.

I don't believe for a second that Adam would've wanted to stay in Sector 45—and risk James's life—if he'd known Anderson was going to be there. Adam can be a dickhead sometimes, but he's spent his whole life trying to protect that ten-year-old from their father. He'd sooner die than put James within close proximity of Anderson—especially after hearing about Anderson's nebulous plans for them. Adam wouldn't do it; he wouldn't risk it. I know this. I know it in my *soul*.

But no one wanted to hear it.

"C'mon, man," Winston said softly. "James isn't your responsibility. Whatever happens to him, this isn't your fault. We have to move on."

It was like I was speaking a foreign language. Screaming at a wall. Everyone thought I was overreacting. Being too emotional. No one wanted to hear my fears.

Eventually, Castle stopped answering my questions. Instead, he started sighing a lot, like he did when I was twelve years old and he caught me trying to hide stray dogs in my bedroom. He shot me a look just before he left tonight—a look that clearly said he felt sorry for me—and I don't know what the hell I'm supposed to do with that.

Even Brendan—kind, compassionate Brendan—shook his head and said, "Adam made his decision. It's been hard for all of us to lose them, Kenji, but you have to let it go."

Fuck that.

I didn't let it go.

I won't let it go.

I look up, homing in on the remains of Warner's massive birthday cake. It's unguarded, sitting on a table in the center of the room, and I'm struck by a sudden urge to put my fist through it. My fingers flex around the fork again, an unconscious impulse I don't bother to examine.

I'm not mad that we're celebrating Warner's birthday. Honestly, I'm not. It's nice, I get it, dude's never had a birthday before. But right now I'm just not in the mood to celebrate. Right now I'd like to punch that piece-of-shit sheet cake and throw it at the wall. I'd like to pick it up and throw it at the wall and then I'd—

Electric heat shoots up my spine and I stiffen, even as I watch, as if from miles away, as a hand curls around my fist. I feel her tugging, trying to pry the fork from my hand. And then I hear her laugh.

I feel suddenly queasier.

"You okay?" she says. "You were holding this thing like a weapon." She sounds like she might be smiling, but I wouldn't know. I'm still staring into space, my vision narrowing into nothing. Nazeera managed to get the fork free of my hand and now I'm just sitting here, my fingers frozen open, still reaching for something.

I feel her sit next to me.

Even from here, I can feel her heat, her presence. I close my eyes. We haven't really talked, she and I. Not about us, anyway. Not about how hard my heart beats when she's around, and definitely not about how she's inspired all the inappropriate daydreams infesting my mind. In fact, since that brief scene in my bedroom, we haven't discussed anything that wasn't strictly professional, and I'm not sure why we would. There's no point.

Kissing her was stupid.

I'm an idiot, Nazeera is probably crazy, and whatever happened between us was a huge mistake. She keeps messing with my head, confusing my emotions, and I keep trying to remind myself, keep trying to convince myself to understand logic—but for some reason my body doesn't get it. The way my biology reacts to her mere *presence*, you'd think I was having a stroke.

Or an aneurysm.

"Hey." Her voice is serious now, the smile gone. "What's wrong?"

I shake my head.

"Don't shake your head at me." She laughs. "You murdered your cake, Kenji. Something is obviously wrong."

At that, I turn an inch. Stare at her out of the corner of my eye.

In response, she rolls her own eyes. "Oh please," she says, stabbing my fork—*my fork*—into the collapsed cake. "Everyone knows you love food. You're always eating. You rarely stop eating long enough to speak."

I blink at her.

She scrapes a bit of frosting off the plate and holds up the fork, like a lollipop, before popping it in her mouth. And only after she's licked the thing clean do I say:

"That fork was in my mouth."

She hesitates. Stares at the cake. "I thought you weren't eating this."

"I'm not eating it *anymore*," I say. "But I took a couple of bites."

And there's something about the way she straightens—something about the mortified way she says, "Of course you did," as she puts down the fork—that unclenches the fist around my spine. Her reaction is so juvenile—as if we haven't already kissed, as if we don't already know what it's like to taste the same things at the same time—that I can't help it. I start laughing.

A moment later, she's laughing, too.

And suddenly I feel almost human again.

I sigh, losing some of the tension in my shoulders. I rest my elbows on the wooden table and drop my head in my hands.

"Hey," she says quietly. "You can tell me, you know."

Her voice is close. Warm. I take a deep breath. "Tell you what?"

"Tell me what's wrong."

I laugh again, but this time the sound is bitter. Nazeera is the last person I want to talk to. It must be some kind of cruel joke that, of all the people I know, she's the one pretending to care.

I sigh as I sit up, frowning into the distance.

I spot Juliette across the room—long brown hair and electric smile—in less than a second. Right now my best friend has eyes only for her boyfriend, and I'm both annoyed and resigned to the fact. I can't blame her for claiming a bit of joy tonight; I know she's been through hell.

But right now I need her, too.

It's been a rough night, and I wanted to talk to her earlier, to ask her what she thinks about the situation with Adam and James, but I'd only made it halfway across the room when Castle pulled me back. He made me promise to leave her alone tonight. He said it was important for J to have alone time with Warner. He wanted them to have a few moments of peace—an uninterrupted night to recover from everything they've been through. I rolled my eyes so hard they nearly fell out of my head.

No one ever gives *me* an uninterrupted night to recover from all the shit I've been through. No one really cares about my emotional state; no one but J, if I'm being honest.

I keep staring at her, my eyes burning holes in her back. I want her to look at me. I know if she could just see me, she'd know something was wrong and she'd come over here. I know she would. But the truth is, it's not just Castle keeping me from ruining her night; after everything they've been through, she and Warner really do deserve a proper reunion. I also think that if I tried to pry her away from Warner right now he'd try to murder me for real.

But sometimes I wonder—

*What about me?*

Why don't my feelings matter? Other people get to experience a full range of emotions without judgment, but I can't be anything but happy without making most people uncomfortable. Everyone is used to seeing me smiling, being goofy. I'm the fun guy, the easygoing guy. I'm the one everyone can count on for a good laugh. When I'm sad or pissed off no one knows what to do with me. I've tried talking to Castle or Winston—even Ian—but no one has ever clicked with me the way J does. Castle always tries his best, but he doesn't approve of wallowing. He gives me thirty seconds to complain before he's offering me a motivational speech, telling me to be strong. Ian, on the other hand, gets itchy when I tell him too much. He tries to be sympathetic, but then he bolts the first chance he gets. Winston listens. He's a good listener, at least. But then, instead of responding to what I just said, he takes a turn talking about all the things he's been dealing with, and even though I understand that he needs to vent, too, by the end of it I feel ten times worse.

But with Juliette—

*Ella?*

With her, it's different. I never even realized just how much I was missing until we really got to know each other. She lets me talk. She doesn't rush me. She doesn't tell me to calm down or feed me bullshit lines or tell me everything will be fine. When I'm trying to get things off my chest she doesn't make the conversation about her or her own problems. She understands. I can tell. She doesn't have to say a word. I can look into her eyes and know she gets it. She gives a shit about me in a way no one else ever has. It's the same thing that makes her a great leader: she genuinely cares about people. She cares about their lives.

"Kenji?"

Nazeera's touching my hand again, but this time I pull away, jerking awkwardly in my seat. And when I finally look up, into her eyes—I'm surprised.

She seems genuinely worried.

"Kenji," she says again. "You're scaring me."

# TWO

I shake my head as I stand, trying my best to look unbothered.

"It's nothing," I say, but I'm still staring out across the room when I say it.

J is laughing at something that pretty boy just said to her, and then he smiles, and she smiles back, and she's still smiling when he leans in and whispers something in her ear and I watch, in real time, as her whole face turns red. And then he's touching her, kissing her here, right in front of everyone and—

I turn away sharply.

I definitely wasn't supposed to see that.

Technically, they're not *right in front of everyone*. There is no *everyone*. There are like five people in this room. And J and Warner are actually as far away from everyone as they could manage, tucked in a corner of the room. I'm pretty sure I just violated their privacy.

Yeah, I should definitely go to bed.

"You're in love with her, aren't you?"

*That* wakes me up.

I spin around. Nazeera is looking at me like she thinks she's some kind of genius, like she's finally figured out the

Secret Mysteries of Kenji.

As if I were that easy to understand.

"I don't know why I didn't see it before," she's saying. "You guys have such a weird, intense relationship." She shakes her head. "Of course you're in love with her."

Jesus. I'm too tired for this.

I move past Nazeera, rolling my eyes as I go. "I am not in love with her."

"I'm pretty sure I know wh—"

"You don't know anything, okay?" I stop. Turn to face her. "You don't know shit about me. Just like I don't know shit about you."

Her eyebrows fly up her forehead. "What's *that* supposed to mean?"

"Don't do that," I say, pointing at her. "Don't pretend to be dumb."

And I'm out the door, halfway down the dimly lit path leading to my tent, when I hear her voice again.

"Are you still mad at me?" she says. "About the thing with Anderson?"

I stop so suddenly I nearly trip. I turn around, and now I'm looking at her, and I can't help it: I laugh out loud, and it sounds crazy. "The *thing* with Anderson? Are you serious? You mean the *thing* where he showed up, back from the dead and ready to murder all of us because you told him where we were? Or do you mean the thing where he killed Dela-lieu? Or wait, maybe you mean the thing where he put all of us in an asylum to rot to death—or maybe it's the thing where you bound, gagged, drugged, and dragged me onto a plane with him all the way to the other side of the goddamn world?"

She moves lightning fast, standing in front of me in seconds. And then, fury making her voice shake: "I did what I did to save your life. I was saving all of your lives. You should be *thanking* me—and instead you're standing here shouting at me like a child, when I single-handedly saved your entire team from certain death." She shakes her head. "You're unbelievable. You have no idea what I risked in order to make that happen, and it's not my fault if you can't understand."

Silence steps between us, pushes us apart.

"You know what's hilarious?" I shake my head, look up at the night sky. "*This*," I say. "This conversation is hilarious."

"Are you drunk?"

"Stop." I turn back, level her with a dark look. "Stop underestimating my mind. You think I'm too dumb to understand the most basic shit about a rescue mission? Of course I understand," I say angrily. "I get that you had to do some shady things in order to make our escape happen. I'm not angry about that. I'm angry right now because you don't know how to *communicate*."

I see it when her face changes. The fire goes out of her eyes; the tension leaves her shoulders. And then she blinks at me—

Confused.

"I don't understand," Nazeera says quietly.

The sun has been dead for hours now, and the dark, winding path is lit only by low lanterns and the diffused light of nearby tents. She's bathed in it. Glowing. More beautiful than ever, which is nothing short of terrifying, to be honest. Her eyes are big and bright and she's staring at me like she's just a girl and I'm just a guy and we're not both just a pair of dumbasses headed directly for the sun. Like we're not both murderers, more or less.

I sigh. Shove a hand through my hair. The fight has left my body and I'm suddenly so exhausted I'm not sure I can keep standing.

"I need to go to bed," I say, and try to move past her.

"Wait—"

She grabs my arm and I nearly jump out of my skin at the sensation. I pull away, unnerved, but she steps forward and suddenly we're standing so close together I can practically feel her breathing. The night is quiet and crisp and she's all I can see in this flickering darkness. I breathe, breathing her in—something subtle, something sweet—and the memory hits me so hard it knocks the air from my lungs.

Her arms around my neck.

Her hands in my hair.

The way she pinned me against the wall, the way our bodies melted together, the way she ran her hands down my chest and told me I was gorgeous. The soft, desperate sounds she made when I kissed her.

I know now how it feels to have her in my arms. I know

what it's like to kiss her, to lick the curve of her lips, to feel her gasp against my neck. I can still taste her, feel the shape of her, strength and softness, under my hands. I'm not even touching her and it's like it's happening again, frame by frame, and I can't stop staring at her mouth because that damn diamond piercing keeps catching the light, and for a moment—for just a moment—I nearly lose my mind and kiss her again.

My head is full of noise, blood rushing to my ears.

She drives me insane. I don't even know why I like her so much. But I have no control over how my body reacts when she's around. It's wild and illogical and I love it. I hate it.

Some nights I fall asleep running back the tapes—her eyes, her hands, her mouth—

But the tapes always end in the same spot.

*"It would never work, you know? We're not—" She makes a motion between our bodies. "We're so different, right?"*

"Kenji?"

Right. Yeah. Shit, I'm tired.

I take a step backward. The cold night air is sharp and bracing, and when I finally meet her eyes again, my head is clear.

But my voice sounds strange when I say, "I should go."

"Wait," Nazeera says again, and puts her hand on my chest.

*Puts her hand on my chest.*

She's got her hand on me like she owns me, like I'm so easily stopped and conquered. A flame of indignation sparks to life inside of me. It's obvious she's used to getting whatever she wants. Either that, or she takes it by force.

I remove her hand from my chest. She doesn't seem to notice.

"I don't understand," she says. "What do you mean I don't know how to communicate? If I didn't tell you anything about the mission, it was because you didn't need to know."

I roll my eyes.

"You think I didn't need to know that you'd given Anderson a heads-up? You think all of us didn't need to know that he was (a) alive, and (b) on his way to murder us? You didn't think of giving Delalieu a warning to shut his mouth just long enough to keep himself from getting murdered?" My frustration is snowballing. "You could've told me that you were going to throw us in the asylum *temporarily*. You could've told me that you were going to drug me—you didn't need to knock me out and kidnap me and let me think I was about to be executed. I would've come voluntarily," I say, my voice growing louder. "I would've *helped* you, goddammit."

But Nazeera is unmoved. Her eyes go cold. "You clearly have no idea what I'm dealing with," she says quietly, "if you really think it was that simple. I couldn't risk—"

"And *you* clearly have no idea how to work in a group," I say, cutting her off. "Which makes you nothing more than a liability."

Her eyes go wide with rage.

"You fly solo, Nazeera. You live by a moral code I don't understand, which basically means you do whatever you want, and you change allegiances whenever it feels right or convenient. You cover your hair sometimes—and only when you think it's safe—because it's rebellious, but there's no real commitment in it. You don't actually align yourself with any group, and you still do whatever your dad tells you to do until you decide, for a little while, that you don't want to listen to The Reestablishment.

"You're unpredictable," I say to her. "All over the place. Today, you're on our side—but what about tomorrow?" I shake my head. "I have no idea what your real motivations are. I never know what you're really thinking. And I can never let my guard down around you—because I have no way of knowing whether you're just using me. I can't trust you."

She stares at me, still as stone, and says nothing for what feels like a century. Finally, she takes a step back. Her eyes are inscrutable.

"You should be careful," she says. "That's a dangerous speech to give to someone you can't trust."

But I'm not buying it. Not this time.

"Bullshit," I say. "If you were going to kill me, you'd have done it a long time ago."

"I might change my mind. Apparently I'm unpredictable. All over the place."

"Whatever," I mutter. "I'm done here."

I shake my head and I'm gone, already walking away, five steps closer to sleep and quiet, when she shouts angrily—

"I opened up to you! I let my guard down around *you*, even if you can't do it for me."

That stops me in my tracks.

I spin around. "When?" I shout back, throwing up my hands in frustration. "When have you ever trusted me? When have you ever opened up to me? Never. No— You just do your own thing, whatever and however you want, consequences be damned, and you expect everyone to be cool with it. Well I call bullshit, okay? I'm not into it."

"I told you about my powers!" she cries, her hands in fists at her sides. "I told you guys everything I knew about Ella and Emmaline!"

I let out a long, exhausted breath. I take a few steps toward her, but only because I don't want to shout anymore.

"I don't know how to explain this," I say, steadying my voice. "I mean, I'm trying. I really am. But I don't know how to— Like, listen, I get that you telling me you can be invisible was a big deal. I get that. But there's a huge difference between you sharing a bunch of classified information with a large group of people and you actually *opening* up to me. I don't— I don't want—" I cut myself off, clenching my teeth too hard. "You know what? Never mind."

"No, go ahead," she says, her own anger barely contained. "Say it. What *don't* you want?"

Finally, I meet her eyes. They're bright. Angry. And I don't know what happens, exactly, but staring at her cuts something loose in my brain. Something unkind. Unfiltered.

"I don't want this sterilized version of you," I say. "I don't want the cold, calculating person you have to be for everyone else. This version of you is cruel and unfeeling and loyal to no one. You're not a nice person, Nazeera. You're mean and condescending and arrogant. But all of that would be tolerable, I swear, if I felt like you had a heart in there somewhere. Because if we're going to be friends—if we're going to be *anything*—I need to be able to trust you. And I don't trust friendships of convenience. I don't trust machines."

Too late, I realize my mistake.

Nazeera looks stunned.

She blinks and blinks, and for one long, excruciating second her stony exterior gives way to raw, trembling emotion that makes her look like a child. She stares up at me and suddenly she looks small—young and scared and small. Her eyes glitter, wet with feeling, and the whole picture is so heartbreaking it hits me hard, like a punch to the gut.

A moment later, it's gone.

She turns away, locks the feelings away, slips the mask back on.

I feel frozen.

I just messed up on some cosmic scale and I don't know how to fix it. I don't know what protocol to follow. I also don't know how or when, exactly, I turned into such a grade A douchebag, but I think hanging out with Warner all the time hasn't done me any favors.

I'm not this guy. I don't make girls cry.

But I don't know how to undo this, either. Maybe if I say nothing. Maybe if I just stand here, blinking at outer space, I can turn back the clock. I don't know. I don't know what's going to happen. I only know that I must be a real piece of shit, because anyone who can make Nazeera Ibrahim cry is probably some kind of monster. I didn't even think Nazeera *could* cry. I didn't know she still did that.

That's how stupid I am.

I just made the daughter of the supreme commander of Asia *cry*.

When she finally faces me, the tears are gone but her voice is cold. Hollow. And it's almost like she can't even believe she's saying the words when she says, "I kissed you. Did you think I was a machine then, too?"

My mind goes suddenly blank. "Maybe?"

I hear her sharp intake of breath. Pain flashes across her face.

Oh my God, I'm worse than stupid.

I'm a bad human being.

I have no idea what's wrong with me. I need to stop talking. I want to not be doing this. Not be here. I want to go back to my room and go to sleep and not be here. But something is broken—my brain, my mouth, my general motor controls.

Worse: I don't know how to get out of here. Where is the eject button for escape from conversations with terrifying, beautiful women?

She says: "You honestly think I would do something like

that—you think I would kiss you like that—just to manipulate you?"

I blink at her.

I feel like I'm trapped in a nightmare. Guilt and confusion and exhaustion and anger fuse together, escalating the chaos in my brain to the point of pain and suddenly, incomprehensibly, my head pops off.

Desperate, stupid—

I can't stop shouting.

"How am I supposed to know what you would or wouldn't do to manipulate someone?" I shout. "How am I supposed to know anything about you? How do I even get to be in the same room as someone like you? This whole situation is *bananas*." I'm still shouting. Still trying to figure out how to calm down. "I mean, not only do you know how to murder me in a thousand different ways, but, considering the fact that you're, like, the most beautiful woman I've ever seen in my life— I mean, yeah, it makes a lot more sense that you were just messing with me than it does for me to believe in some alternate universe where you actually find me attractive."

"You are *unbelievable!*"

"And you're clearly insane."

Her mouth falls open. Literally falls open. And for a second she looks so angry I think she might actually rip the throat out of my body.

I backtrack.

"Okay, I'm sorry—you're not insane—but twenty

minutes ago you were accusing me of being in love with my best friend, so, to be fair, I think my feelings are warranted."

"You were looking at her like you were in love with her!"

"Jesus Christ, woman, I look at *you* like I'm in love with you!"

"I— Wait. What?"

I squeeze my eyes shut. "Nothing. Never mind. I have to go."

"Kenji—"

But I'm already gone.

# THREE

When I get back to my room I shut the door and sag against it, sinking to the floor in a sad, pathetic heap. I drop my head into my hands and, in a jarring moment, I think—

I wish my mom were here.

The feeling sideswipes me so fast I can't stop it in time. It grows quickly, spiraling out of control: sadness breeding sadness, self-pity circling me mercilessly. All my shitty experiences—every heartbreak, every disappointment— choose this minute to tear me open, dining out on my heart until there's nothing left, until the grief eats me alive.

I crumble under the weight of it.

I duck my head into my knees, wrap my arms around my shins. Shocks of pain unfurl in my chest, fingers breaking through my rib cage, closing around my lungs.

I can't catch my breath.

At first, I don't feel the tears running down my face. At first I just hear my breathing, harsh and gasping, and I don't understand the sound. I lift my head, stunned, and force out a laugh but it feels foreign, stupid. I'm stupid. I press my fists against my eyes and grit my teeth, driving the tears back into my skull.

I don't know what's wrong with me tonight.

I feel off, unbalanced. Aching for something. I'm losing sight of my purpose, my sense of direction. I always tell myself that I'm fighting every day for hope, for the salvation of humanity, but every time I survive only to return to yet more loss and devastation, something comes loose inside of me. It's like the people and places I love are the nuts and bolts keeping me upright; without them, I'm just scrap metal.

I sigh, long and shaky. Drop my face in my hands.

I almost never allow myself to think about my mom. Almost never. But right now, something about the darkness, the cold, the fear, and the guilt—my confusion over Nazeera—

I wish I could talk to my mom.

I wish she were here to hold me, guide me. I wish I could crawl into her arms like I used to, I wish I could feel her fingers against my scalp at the end of a long night, massaging away the tension. When I had nightmares, or when Dad was gone too long looking for work, she and I would stay up together, holding each other. I'd cling to her and she'd rock me gently, running her fingers through my hair, whispering jokes in my ear. She was the funniest person I ever knew. So smart. So sharp.

God, I miss her.

Sometimes I miss her so much I think my chest is caving in. I feel like I'm sinking in the feeling, like I might never come up for air. And sometimes I think I could just die there, in those moments, violently drowned by emotion.

But then, miraculously—inch by inch—the feeling abates. It's slow, excruciating work, but eventually the cataract clears, and somehow I'm alive again. Alone again.

Here, in the dark, with my memories.

Sometimes I feel so alone in this world I can't even breathe.

Castle's got his kid back. My friends have all found their partners. We've lost Adam. Lost James. Lost everyone else from Omega Point, too. It still hits me sometimes. Still knocks me over when I forget to bury the feelings deep enough.

But I can't keep going like this. I'm falling apart, and I don't have time to fall apart. People need me, depend on me.

I have to get my shit together.

I drag myself up, bracing my back against the door as I find my footing. I've been sitting in the dark, in the cold, in the same clothes I've been wearing for a week. I'll be all right; I just need a change of pace.

James and Adam are probably fine.

They've got to be.

I head to the bathroom, hitting light switches as I go, and turn on the water. I strip off these old clothes, promising to set them on fire as soon as I can, and pull open a few drawers, sifting through the amenities and cotton basics Nouria said would be stocked in our rooms. Satisfied, I step in the shower. I don't know how they got hot water here, and I don't care.

This is perfect.

I lean against the cold tile as the hot water slaps me in the face. Eventually I sink to the floor, too tired to stand.

I let the heat boil me alive.

# FOUR

I thought the shower would perform some kind of restorative cure, but it didn't work as well as I hoped. I feel clean, which is worth something, but I still feel bad. Like, physically bad. I think I've got a better handle on my emotions, but— I don't know.

I think I'm delirious. Or jet-lagged. Or both.

That has to be it.

I'm so exhausted you'd think I would've fallen asleep the second my head hit the pillow, but no such luck. I spent a couple of hours lying in bed, staring at the ceiling, and then I walked around in the dark for a little while, and now I'm here again, throwing a pair of balled-up socks at the wall while the sun makes lazy moves toward the moon.

There's a sliver of light creeping up the horizon. The beginnings of dawn. I'm staring at the scene through the square of my window, still trying to figure out what the hell is wrong with me, when a sudden, violent banging on my door sends a direct shot of adrenaline to my brain.

I'm on my feet in seconds, heart pounding, head pounding. I pull on clothes and boots so fast I nearly kill myself in the process, but when I finally pull the door open, Brendan looks relieved.

"Good," he says. "You're dressed."

"What's wrong?" I ask automatically.

Brendan sighs. He looks sad—and then, for just a second:

He looks scared.

"What's wrong?" I ask again. Adrenaline is moving through me now, dousing my fear. I feel calmer. Sharper. "What happened?"

Brendan hesitates; glances at something over his shoulder. "I'm just a messenger, mate. I'm not supposed to tell you anything."

"What? Why not?"

"Trust me," he says, meeting my eyes. "It'll help to hear this from Castle himself."

# FIVE

"Why?" is the first thing I say to Castle.

I burst through the doorway with maybe a little too much force, but I can't help it. I'm freaking out. "Why do I have to hear this directly from you?" I ask. "What's going on?"

I can hardly keep the anger out of my voice. I can hardly keep myself from imagining every possible worst-case scenario. Any number of horrible things could've happened to merit dragging me out of bed before dawn, and making me wait even five extra minutes to find out what the hell is going on is nothing short of cruel.

Castle stares at me, his face grim, and I take a deep breath, look around, steady my pulse. I have no idea where I am. This looks like some kind of . . . headquarters. Another building. Castle, Sam, and Nouria are seated at a long wooden table, atop which are scattered papers, waterlogged blueprints, a ruler, three pocketknives, and several old cups of coffee.

"Sit down, Kenji."

But I'm still looking around, this time searching for J. Ian and Lily are here. Brendan and Winston, too.

No J. No Warner. And no one is making eye contact with me.

"Where's Juliette?" I ask.

"You mean Ella," Castle says gently.

"Whatever. Why isn't she here?"

"Kenji," Castle says. "Please sit down. This is hard enough without having to manage your emotions, too. Please."

"With all due respect, sir, I'll sit down after I know what the hell is going on."

Castle sighs heavily. Finally, he says—

"You were right."

My eyes widen, my heart still hammering in my chest. "Excuse me?"

"You were right," Castle says, and his voice catches on the last word. He clenches and unclenches his fists. "About Adam. And James."

But I'm shaking my head. "I don't want to be right. I was overreacting. They're fine. Don't listen to me," I say, sounding a little crazy. "I'm not right. I'm never right."

"Kenji."

"*No.*"

Castle looks up, looks me directly in the eye. He looks devastated. Beyond devastated.

"Tell me this is a joke," I say.

"Anderson has taken the boys hostage," he says, glancing at Brendan and Winston. Ian. The ghost of Emory. "He's doing it again."

I can't handle this.

My heart can't handle this. I'm already too close to the edge of crisis. This is too much. *Too much.*

"You're wrong," I insist. "Anderson wouldn't do that, not to James. James is just a child— He wouldn't do that to a child—"

"Yes," Winston says quietly. "He would."

I glance over at him, my eyes wild. I feel stupid. I feel like my skin is too tight. Too loose. And I'm looking at Castle again when I say:

"How do you know? How can you be sure this isn't another trap, just like last time—"

"Of course it's a trap," Nouria says. Her voice is firm but not unkind. She glances at Castle before she says: "I'm not sure why, but my dad is making this sound like a simple hostage situation. It's not. We're not even sure exactly what's happening yet. It definitely looks like Anderson is holding the boys hostage, but it's also clear that there's something much bigger happening behind the scenes. Anderson is plotting something. If he weren't, he wouldn't have—"

"I think," Sam says, squeezing her wife's hand, "what Nouria is trying to say is that we think Adam and James play only a small role in all of this."

I glance between them, confused. There's tension in the room that wasn't there a moment ago, but my head feels too full of sand to figure it out. "I don't think I understand what you're getting at," I say.

But it's Castle who explains.

"It's not just Adam and James," he says. "Anderson currently has custody of all the kids—specifically, the children of the supreme commanders."

And I'm about to ask another question before I realize—

I'm the *only* one asking questions right now. I glance around the room, at the faces of my friends. They look sad but determined. Like they already know how this story ends, and they're ready to face it.

I'm floored by the revelation. And I can't keep the edge out of my voice when I say, "Why was I the last to be informed about this?"

My question is followed by perfect silence. Harried glances. Nervous expressions.

Then, finally:

"We knew it would be hard for you," Lily says. Lily, who never gives a shit about my feelings. "You'd just been on this crazy mission, and then we had to shoot your plane out of the sky— Honestly, we weren't sure if we should tell you right away." She hesitates. And then, aiming an irritated look at the other ladies in the room: "But if it makes you feel any better, Nouria and Sam didn't tell *us* right away, either."

"What?" My eyebrows fly up my head. "What the hell is going on? When did you first get the news?"

The room goes quiet again.

"*When?*" I demand.

"Fourteen hours ago," Nouria says.

"*Fourteen hours ago?*" My eyes widen to the point of pain. "You knew about this *fourteen hours ago* and you're only telling me now? Castle?"

He shakes his head.

"They kept it from me, too," he says, and despite his calm demeanor, I notice the tension in his jaw. He won't look me in the eye. He won't look at Nouria, either.

Realization dawns with sudden, startling speed, and I finally understand: there are too many cooks in this metaphorical kitchen.

I had no idea what kind of complicated shitshow I'd just walked into, but it's clear that Nouria and Sam are used to running this place on their own. Daughter or not, Nouria is the head of this resistance, and it doesn't matter how much she likes having her dad around, she's not about to cede control. Which apparently means she's going to keep him from accessing classified information before she deems it necessary. Which means— Hell, I think it means Castle has no real authority anymore.

Holy shit.

"So you knew about this," I say, looking from Nouria to Sam. "You knew it when we landed here yesterday—you knew then that Anderson was rounding up the kids. When we had cake and sang happy birthday to Warner, you knew that James and Adam had been abducted. When I asked, over and over and over again, why the hell Adam and James weren't here, you knew and *said nothing*—"

"Calm down," Nouria says sharply. "You're losing control."

"How could you lie to us like that?" I demand, not bothering to keep my voice down. "How could you stand there and smile when you knew our friends were suffering?"

"Because we had to be sure," Sam says to me. And then she sighs, heavily, pushing wisps of her blond hair out of her face. There are purple smudges under her eyes that tell me I'm not the only one who's been losing sleep lately. "Anderson had his men feed this information directly underground. He planted it in our networks on purpose, which made me doubt his motives from the start.

"Anderson seems to have figured out that your team took refuge with another rebel group," she says. "But he doesn't know which of us is protecting you. I figured he was just trying to lure us out, into the open, so I wanted to verify the information before we spread it any further. We didn't want to take next steps without being certain, and we didn't think it would be good for morale to spread hurtful information that might, ultimately, be false."

"You waited fourteen hours to spread information that might've been *true*," I cry. "Anderson could've decided to kill them off by now!"

Nouria shakes her head. "That's not how a hostage situation works. He's made it clear he wants something from us. He wouldn't kill off his own bargaining chips."

I go suddenly still. "What do you mean? What does he want from us?" Then, looking around again: "And why the hell isn't Juliette here right now? She needs to be hearing this."

"There's no reason to disturb Ella's sleep," Sam says, "because there's nothing we can do at the moment. We'll fill her in in the morning."

"The hell we are," I say angrily, forgetting myself. "I'm sorry, sir, I know we're not at Point anymore, but you have to do something. This isn't okay. J led a goddamn resistance—she doesn't want to be coddled or protected from this shit. And when she finds out that we didn't tell her she's going to be pissed."

"Kenji—"

"This is all some sort of bullshit, anyway," I say, my hands caught in my hair. "A bluff. More lies. There's no way Anderson has all the other kids. He's obviously trying to mess with our heads—and it's working—because he knows we could never be sure whether he's actually taken them hostage. This is all some complicated mind game," I say. "It's the perfect play."

"It's not," Brendan says, putting his hand on my shoulder. His eyebrows pull together with concern. "It's not a mind game."

"Of course it—"

"Sam saw them," Nouria says. "We have proof."

I stiffen. "What?"

"I can see across long distances," Sam says. She tries to smile, but she just looks tired. "Really, really long distances. We figured if Anderson was going to take the kids anywhere he'd do it somewhere close to his home base, where he has soldiers and resources at his disposal. And when Ella told us Evie was dead, I felt even more certain that he'd head back to North America, where he'd need to do damage control and maintain his power over the continent. In the event that another rebel group tried to take advantage of the sudden upheaval, he'd have to be here, exercise his power, maintain order. So I focused on Sector 45 in my search. It took nearly all fourteen hours to do a proper sweep, but I'm certain I've found enough evidence to support his claims."

"What the hell kind of— You're certain you've found *enough* evidence? What kind of vague nonsense is that? And why are you the one who gets to decide wh—"

"Watch your tone, Kishimoto," Nouria says sharply. "Sam has been working nonstop trying to figure this situation out. You will recognize her authority here, where we've offered you refuge, and you will give her your gratitude and your respect."

Sam places a calming hand on Nouria's arm. "It's all right," Sam says, still looking at me. "He's just overset."

"We're all overset," Nouria says, narrowing her eyes at me. Anger gives her a sudden, ethereal glow that makes her dark skin seem almost bioluminescent. For a moment, I can't look away.

I give my head a quick shake to clear it.

"I'm not trying to be disrespectful," I say. "I just don't understand why we're buying into this. 'Enough evidence' doesn't sound convincing, especially not when Anderson pulled this exact same shit before. Do you remember how that turned out? If it weren't for J, who saved all our asses that day, we'd be dead. Ian would definitely be dead right now."

113

"Yes," Castle says patiently, "but you're forgetting one important detail."

I tilt my head at him.

"Anderson did indeed have our men. He never lied about that."

I clench my jaw. My fists. My whole body turns to stone.

"Denial is the first stage of grief, bro."

"Fuck off, Sanchez."

"That is *enough*," Castle says, standing up with sudden force. He looks livid, the table rattling under his splayed fingers. "What's the matter with you, son? This isn't like you—this angry, reckless, disrespectful behavior. Your harsh judgments are doing nothing to help the current situation."

I squeeze my eyes shut.

Anger explodes in the blackness behind my eyelids, fireworks building and breaking me down.

My head is spinning.

My heart is spinning.

A bead of sweat travels down my back and I shiver, involuntarily.

"Fine," I snap, opening my eyes. "I apologize for my disrespectful behavior. But I'm only going to ask this question one more time before I go and get her myself: Why the hell isn't Juliette here right now?"

Their collective silence is the only answer I need.

"What is really going on?" I say angrily. "Why are you doing this? Why are you letting her sleep and rest and recover so much? What aren't you telling m—"

114

"Kenji." Castle sounds suddenly different. His eyes are pulled together, his forehead creased in concern. "Are you feeling all right?"

I blink. Take a sudden, steadying breath. "I'm fine," I say, but for a second the words sound strange, like I got caught in an echo.

"Bro, you don't look okay."

Who said that?

Ian?

I turn toward his voice, but everything seems to warp as I move, sounds bending in half.

"Yeah, maybe you should get some sleep."

Winston?

I turn again, and this time all the sounds speed up, fast-forwarding until they collide in real time. My ears start ringing. And then I look down, realizing too late that my hands are shaking. My teeth are shaking. Chattering. I'm *freezing*. "Why is it so cold in here?" I ask.

Brendan is suddenly standing next to me. "Let me take you back to your room," he says. "Maybe y—"

"I'm fine," I lie, lurching away from him. I can feel my heart racing too fast, the movement so quick it's a blur, practically a vibration.

It freaks me out.

I need to calm down. I need to catch my breath. I need to sit—or lean against something—

Exhaustion hits me like a bullet between the eyes. Suddenly, ferociously, digging its claws into my chest and dragging me down. I stumble over to a chair, blinking slowly. My arms feel heavy. My heart rate begins to slow. I'm liquid.

My eyes fall closed.

Instantly, an image of James materializes in my mind: hungry, bruised, beaten. Alone and terrified.

Horror sends an electric shock to my heart, brings me back to life.

My eyes fly open.

"Listen." My throat is dry. I swallow, hard. "Listen," I say again, "if this is true, if James and Adam are really being held hostage by Anderson right now, then we have to go. We have to go right now. Right the hell *now*—"

"Kenji, we can't," Sam says. She's standing in front of me, which surprises me. "We can't do anything right now." She's pronouncing the words slowly. Carefully, like she's talking to a child.

"Why not?"

"Because we don't know yet exactly where they are." Nouria, this time. "And because you're right: this whole thing is some kind of a trap."

She's looking at me like she feels sorry for me, and it sends another shot of anger through my blood. "We can't go into this unprepared," she says. "We need more time. More information."

"We're going to get them back," Castle says, stepping forward. He drops his hands on my shoulders, peers into my face. "I swear to you we'll get them back. James and Adam are going to be fine. We just need to form a plan first."

116

"No," I say angrily, breaking away. "None of this makes sense. Juliette needs to be here. This whole situation is fucked."

"*Kenji—*"

I storm out of the room.

# SIX

I must be out of my mind.

That's got to be it. There's no other reason why I'd swear in Castle's face, scream at his daughter, fight my own friends, and still be standing here at dawn, pressing this doorbell for the third time. It's like I'm *asking* to be murdered. It's like I want Warner to just punch me in the face or something. Even now, through the thick, dumb fog of my head, I know I shouldn't be here. I know it's not right.

But I'm either (a) too stupid, (b) too tired, (c) too angry, or (d) all of the above, to give a proper shit about their personal space or their privacy. And then, as if on cue, I hear his muffled, angry voice through the door.

"Please, love. Just ignore it."

"What if something's wrong?"

"Nothing is wrong," he says. "It's just Kenji."

"Kenji?" I hear some kind of shuffle, and my heart picks up. J always comes through. She *always* comes through. "How do you know it's Kenji?"

"Call it a wild guess," Warner says.

I ring the doorbell again.

"Coming!" J. Finally.

"She's *not* coming," Warner shouts. "Go away."

"I'm not going anywhere," I shout back. "I want to talk to Juliette. Ella. Jella. Jello. Whatever."

"Ella, love, please—let me kill him."

I hear J laugh, which is sweet, actually, because it's clear she thinks Warner's joking. Me, on the other hand—I'm pretty sure he's not.

Warner says something then, something I don't hear. The room goes quiet, and, for a moment, I'm confused. And then I realize I've been bested. Warner probably got her back into bed.

*Goddammit.*

"But that's exactly why I should answer the door," I hear her say. More silence. Then rustling. A muted thud. "If he needs to talk to me this early in the morning, it must be important."

Warner sighs so loudly I actually hear it through the wall.

I press the doorbell again.

A single, unintelligible cry.

"*Hey,*" I call out. "Seriously—someone open the door. I'm freezing my ass off out here."

More angry mutters from Warner.

"I'll be right there," Jello shouts.

"What's taking so long?" I ask.

"I'm trying to—" I hear her laugh, and then, in a soft, sweet voice clearly directed at someone else: "Aaron, please—I promise I'll be right back."

"J?"

"I'm trying to get dressed!"

"*Oh*." I try really, really hard not to picture them both, undressed, in bed together, but somehow I can't fight the image from materializing. "Okay, ew."

Then: "Sweetheart, how long do you plan on being friends with him?"

J laughs again.

Man, that girl has no clue.

I mean, okay . . . It's true that if for five seconds I stopped to put myself in Warner's shoes, I'd understand exactly why he wants to kill me so often. If I were in bed with my girl and some needy asshole kept ringing the doorbell for no reason except that he wanted to talk through his feelings with her, I'd want to murder him, too.

Then again, I don't have a girl, and at this rate, I probably never will. So I kind of don't care—and Warner knows that. It's half the reason he hates me so much. He can't push me away without hurting J, but he can't let me in without sharing her, either. He's in a shitty position.

Works out for me, though.

And I've still got my finger hovering over the doorbell when I hear footsteps, growing closer. But when the door finally flies open, I take a sudden, jerky step back.

Warner looks furious.

His hair is disheveled, the sash on his robe tied too quickly. He's shirtless, barefoot, and probably naked under that robe, which is the only reason I force myself to meet his eyes.

*Shit.*

He wasn't joking even a little bit. He's, like, genuinely pissed.

And his voice is low—lethal—when he says, "I should've let you freeze to death in Kent's old apartment. I should've let those rodents devour your carefully preserved carcass. I should've—"

"Listen, man, I'm really not trying to—"

"*Don't* interrupt me."

My mouth snaps shut.

He takes a sharp, steady breath. His eyes are like fire. Green. Ice. Fire. In that order. "Why do you do this to me? Why?"

"Um. Okay, I know this will be hard for a narcissist like you to understand, but this has nothing to do with you. J is my friend. In fact, she was my friend first. We were friends long before you ever came around."

Warner's eyes widen with outrage. And before he has a chance to speak, I say—

"My bad. I'm sorry." I hold up my hands in apology. "I forgot about the whole memory-wiping thing for a second. But honestly, whatever. As far as *my* memories are concerned, I knew her first."

And then, all of a sudden—

Warner frowns.

It's like someone hits a switch, and the fire in his eyes goes out. He's studying me closely now, and it's making me nervous.

"What's going on?" he says. He tilts his head at me, and, a moment later, his eyes widen in surprise. "Why are you terrified?"

Jello shows up before I can answer.

She smiles at me—this big, bright, happy thing that always warms my heart—and I'm relieved to discover that she's fully clothed. Not naked-under-a-bathrobe-clothed, but, like, she's wearing a coat and shoes and she's ready to walk out the door kind of clothed.

I feel like I can finally breathe.

But in an instant, her smile is gone. And when she goes suddenly pale, when her eyes pull together in concern—I feel the tiniest bit better. I know it sounds strange, but there's something reassuring about her reaction; it means that at least something is right with the world. Because I *knew*. I knew that, unlike everyone else, she'd see right away that I wasn't okay. That I'm not okay. No superpowers necessary.

And somehow, that means everything.

"Kenji," she says, "what's wrong?"

I can hardly hold it together anymore. A dull, throbbing pain is pressing against the back of my left eye; black spots fade in and out of my vision, pockmarking everything. I feel like I can't get enough air, like my chest is too small, my brain too big.

"Kenji?"

"It's James," I say, my voice coming out thin. Wrong. "Anderson took him. Anderson took James and Adam. He's holding them hostage."

# SEVEN

We're back in the war room.

I'm standing at the door with J by my side—Warner needed a minute to pick out a cute outfit and braid his hair—and in the fifteen minutes I was gone, the atmosphere in this room changed dramatically. Everyone keeps glancing between me and J. Glaring, more like. Brendan looks tired. Winston looks irritated. Ian looks pissed. Lily looks pissed. Sam looks pissed. Nouria looks pissed.

Castle looks *super* pissed.

He's staring at me through narrowed eyes, and our years together have taught me enough about Castle's body language to know exactly what he's thinking right now.

Right now, he's thinking that he's more than a little disappointed in me, that he feels betrayed by my reneging on a promise to stop using the f-word, that I deliberately disrespected him, and that I should be grounded for two weeks for shouting at his daughter and her wife. Also, he's embarrassed. He expected more from me.

"I'm sorry I lost my temper, sir."

Castle's jaw tenses as he appraises me. "Are you feeling better?"

No. "Yes."

"Then we'll discuss this later."

I look away, too tired to drum up the necessary remorse. I'm too spent. Depleted. Wrung out. I feel like my insides have been scraped out with blunt, rusted tools, but somehow I'm still here. Still standing. Somehow, having J by my side is making this whole thing more tolerable. It feels good to know that there's someone here who's on my team.

After a full minute of awkward silence, J speaks.

"So," she says, letting the word hang in the air for a moment. "Why didn't anyone tell me about this meeting?"

"We didn't want to disturb you," Nouria says too sweetly. "You've had such a rough couple of weeks—we figured it best not to wake you unless we had a firm plan of action."

J frowns. I can tell she's considering—and doubting—what Nouria just said to her. It sounds like bullshit to me, too. We pretty much never make special arrangements to let people rest or sleep after a battle—not unless they're injured. Sometimes, not even then. J, in particular, has never been given special treatment like this before. We don't treat her like a child, handling her like she's made of porcelain. Like she might still shatter.

But Jello decides to let it go.

"I realize you were trying to be kind," she says to Nouria, "and I'm grateful for the space and generosity—especially last night, for Aaron—but you should've told us right away. In fact, you should've told us the minute we landed. It doesn't matter how much we've been through," she says. "Our heads are here, in the reality of what we're dealing with right now, and Aaron is going to be fighting alongside us. It's time for all of you to stop underestimating him."

"Wait— What?" Ian frowns. "What does underestimating Warner have to do with James?"

J shakes her head. "Aaron has everything to do with James. In fact," she says, "I can't understand why he wasn't the first person you talked to about this. Your biases are hurting you. Holding you back."

It's my turn to frown. "What's the point of this speech, princess? I don't see how Warner is relevant to the conversation. And why do you keep calling him Aaron? It's weird."

"I— *Oh*," she says, and frowns. "I'm sorry. My mind— My memories are still . . . I'm having a hard time. He's been Aaron to me much longer than he was ever Warner."

I raise an eyebrow. "I think I'll stick to calling him Warner."

"I think he'd prefer that from you."

"Good. Anyway. So you think we underestimate him."

"I do," she says.

This time, Nouria speaks up. "And why is that?"

J exhales. Her eyes are both sad and serious when she says:

"Anderson is the kind of monster who'd take hostage a ten-year-old boy and throw him in prison alongside trained soldiers. As far as we know, he's treating James the same way he's treating Valentina. Or Lena. Or Adam. It's inhumane on a level so disturbing I can hardly allow myself to think about it. It's hard for me to fathom. But it's not hard for Aaron to imagine. He knows Anderson—and the inner workings of his mind—better than any of us. His knowledge of The Reestablishment and Anderson, in particular, is priceless.

"More important: James is Aaron's little brother. And if anyone knows what it's like to be ten years old and tortured by Anderson, it's Aaron." She looks up, looks Castle directly in the eye. "How could you think leaving him out of this conversation was a good idea? How could you imagine he wouldn't be the first to care? He's devastated."

And then, as if she conjured him out of thin air, Warner appears at the door. I blink, and Nazeera is following him into the room. I blink again, and Haider and Stephan come into view.

It's weird, seeing them together like this, all of them little science experiments. Super soldiers. They all walk the same, tall and proud, perfect posture, looking like they own the world.

Which, I guess they kind of do. At least, their parents do. *Bizarre.*

I can't imagine what it must be like to be raised by parents who teach you that the world is yours to do with what you will. Maybe Nazeera was right. Maybe we are too different. Maybe it never would've worked out between us, no matter how much I would've wanted to give it a shot.

Nazeera, Stephan, and Haider give us a wide berth, standing off to the side and saying nothing—not even waving hello—but Warner keeps walking. Jello meets him in the middle of the room, and he pulls her into his arms like they haven't seen each other in days. Somehow, I manage not to vomit. But then I hear her whisper something about his birthday, and a massive wave of guilt washes over me.

I can't believe I forgot.

We were celebrating Warner's birthday a little prematurely last night. Today is his proper birthday. Today. Right now. This morning.

Shit.

I dragged J out of bed on the morning of his *birthday*.

Wow, I really am an asshole.

When they break apart, Warner makes a sudden, almost imperceptible motion with his head and Nazeera, Stephan, and Haider make their way over to the table, taking their seats alongside Ian and Lily and Brendan and Winston. A little battalion ready for war. Sometimes it's hard to believe we're all just a bunch of kids. It definitely doesn't feel like it. But these four, in particular—they look pretty damn striking.

Warner is wearing a leather jacket. I've never seen him wear a leather jacket before, and I don't know why. It suits him. It has an interesting, complicated collar, and the black of the leather is stark against his gold hair. But the more I think about it, the more I doubt the jacket belongs to him. We had no possessions when we landed here, so I'm guessing Warner borrowed it from Haider. Haider, who's wearing one of his signature chain-mail shirts under a heavy wool coat. But all of that is nothing compared to Stephan, who's wearing a gold field jacket that looks like snakeskin.

It's wild.

These guys look almost like aliens here, among the normals of the world who don't wear chain mail to breakfast. But even I can tell that Haider looks like some kind of warrior with all that metal draped across his chest, and that the gold jacket really pops against the brown of Stephan's skin. But who sells shit like that? They're like outer-space clothes or something. I have no idea where these guys do their shopping, but I think they might be going to the wrong stores. Then again, what the hell would I know. I've been wearing the same ripped pants and shirts for years. Everything I once owned was faded and poorly mended and a little too tight, if I'm being honest. I considered myself lucky to have one good winter coat and a decent pair of boots. That's it.

"Kenji?"

I startle, realizing too late that I got lost in my head again. Someone is talking to me. Someone said my name. Right? I glance at their faces, hoping for recognition, but I get nothing.

I look to J for help, and she smiles. "Nazeera," she explains, "just asked you a question."

Shit.

I was ignoring Nazeera. On purpose. I thought that was obvious. I thought she and I had an understanding—I thought we'd entered into a silent agreement to ignore each other forever, to never acknowledge the dumb shit I said last night, and to pretend that I can't feel the blood rush to all the wrong places in my body when she touches me.

No?

Okay then.

Shit.

Reluctantly, I turn to look at her. She's wearing that leather hood of hers again, which means I can see only her lips, which seems really, really unfair. She has a gorgeous mouth. Full. Sweet. Damn. I don't want to stare at her mouth. I mean, I do, obviously. But I also definitely don't. Anyway, it's hard enough to have to keep staring at her mouth, but her hood is hiding her eyes, which means I have no idea what she's thinking right now, or if she's still mad at me for what I said last night.

Then—

"I was asking if you'd suspected anything," Nazeera says. "About James. And Adam."

How did I miss that? How long did I spend staring into space thinking about where Haider does his shopping?

Jesus.

What the hell is wrong with me?

I give my head a slight shake, hoping to clear it. "Yeah," I say. "I kind of freaked out about it when we showed up here and I didn't see Adam and James. I told everyone, too," I say, shooting individual glares at my useless friends, "but no one listened to me. Everyone thought I was crazy."

Nazeera pulls back her hood, and for the first time this morning, I can see her face. I search her eyes, but I get nothing. Her expression is clear. There's nothing in her tone or posture to tell me what she's really thinking.

Nothing.

And then her eyes narrow, just a tiny bit. "You told everyone."

"I mean"—I blink, hesitate—"I told some people. Yeah."

"You didn't tell any of us, though." She gestures at the little group of mercenaries. "You didn't tell Ella or Warner. Or the rest of us."

"Castle said I wasn't supposed to tell you guys," I say, glancing between J and Warner. "He wanted you to be able to have a nice evening together."

J is about to say something, but Nazeera cuts her off.

"Yes, I understand that," she says, "but did he also tell you not to say anything to Haider and Stephan? To me? Castle didn't say that you had to withhold your suspicions from the rest of us, did he?"

There's no inflection in her voice. No anger, not even a hint of irritation—but everyone turns suddenly to look at her. Haider's eyebrows are raised. Even Warner looks curious.

Apparently, Nazeera is being weird.

But exhaustion has crashed into me again.

Somehow, I know this is the end. I'm out of lives. No more power-ups. There won't be any more bursts of anger or adrenaline to push me through another minute. I try to speak, but the wires in my brain have been disconnected, rerouted.

My mouth opens. Closes.

Nothing.

This time the exhaustion drives into me with such violent force I feel like my bones are cracking, like my eyes are melting, like I'm looking at the world through cellophane. Everything takes on a slightly metallic sheen, glassy and blurred. And then, for the first time, I realize—

This doesn't feel like normal exhaustion.

It's too late, though. Way too late to realize that I might be more than just really, really tired.

Hell, I think I might be dying.

Stephan says something. I don't hear him.

Nazeera says something. I don't hear her.

Some still-functioning part of my brain tells me to go back to my room and die in peace, but when I try to take a step forward, I stumble.

Weird.

I take another step forward, but this time, it's worse. My legs tangle and I trip, only catching myself at the last moment.

Everything feels wrong.

The sounds in my head seem to be getting louder. I can't open my eyes fully. The air around me feels tight—compressed—and I try to say *I feel so strange* but it's useless. All I know is that I feel suddenly cold. Freezing hot.

Wait. That's not right.

I frown.

"Kenji?"

The word comes to me from far away. Underwater. My eyes are closed now, and it feels like they'll stay that way forever. And then— Everything smells different. Like dirt and wet and cold. Weird. Something is tickling my face. Grass? When did I get grass on my face?

"*Kenji!*"

Oh. *Oh.* Not cool. Someone is shaking me, hard, rattling my brain around in my skull and something, some ancient instinct, pries the rusted hinges of my eyelids open, but when I try to focus, I can't. Everything is soft. Mushy.

Someone is shouting. Someone*s*. Wait, what's the plural of *someone*? I don't think I've ever heard so many people say my name at the same time. Kenji kenji kenji kenjikenjikenji

I try to laugh.

And then I see her. There she is. Man, this is a nice dream. But there she is. She's touching my face. I turn my head a little, rest my cheek against the smooth, soft palm of her hand. It feels amazing.

Nazeera.

*So fucking beautiful,* I think.

And then I'm gone.

Weightless.

# EIGHT

When I open my eyes, I see spiders.

Eyes and arms, eyes and arms, eyes and arms everywhere. Magnified. Up close. A thousand eyes, round and shining. Hundreds of arms reaching toward me, around me.

I close my eyes again.

It's a good thing I'm not afraid of spiders, otherwise I think I'd be screaming. But I've learned to live with spiders. I lived with them in the orphanage, on the streets at night, underground at Omega Point. They hide in my shoes, under my bed, capture flies in the corners of my room. I usually nudge them back outside, but I never kill them. We have an understanding, spiders and I. We're cool.

But I've never *heard* spiders before.

And these things are loud. It's a lot of discordant noise, a lot of humming, vibrating nonsense I can't separate into sounds. But then, slowly, they begin to separate. Find forms.

I realize they're voices.

"You're right that it's unusual," someone says. "It's definitely strange that he'd be experiencing any lingering effects this long afterward—but it's not unheard of."

"That theory makes no sense—"

"*Nazeera.*" That sounds like Haider. "These are their

healers. I'm sure they would know what—"

"I don't care," she says sharply. "I happen to disagree. Kenji's been fine these last couple of days, and I would know; I was with him. This is an absurd diagnosis. It's irresponsible to suggest that he's being affected by drugs that were administered *days* ago, when the underlying cause is unequivocally something else."

There's a long stretch of silence.

Finally, I hear someone sigh.

"You may find this hard to believe, but what we do isn't magic. We deal in actual science. We can, within certain parameters, heal an ill or injured person. We can regrow tissue and bone and replenish blood loss, but we can't do much for . . . food poisoning, for example. Or a hangover. Or chronic exhaustion. There are still many ills and illnesses we can't yet cure." That must be Sara. Or Sonya. Or both. I can't always tell their voices apart.

"And right now," one of them says, "despite our best efforts, Kenji still has these drugs in his system. They have to run their course."

"But— There has to be something—"

"Kenji's been running on pure adrenaline these last thirty-six hours," one of the twins says. "The highs and lows are devastating his body, and sleep deprivation is making him more susceptible to the effects of the drugs."

"Is he going to be okay?" Nazeera asks.

"Not if he doesn't sleep."

"What does that mean?" J. Jella. Jello. That's her voice.

She sounds terrified. "How serious is the damage? How long could it take for him to recover?"

And then, as my mind continues to sharpen, I realize that the twins are talking in tandem, completing each other's thoughts and sentences so it seems like only one person is speaking. That makes more sense.

Sara: "We can't know for certain."

Sonya: "It might be hours, it might be days."

"*Days?*" Nazeera again.

Sara: "Or not. It really just depends on the strength of his immune system. He's young and otherwise very healthy, so he has the best chance of bouncing back. But he's severely dehydrated."

Sonya: "And he needs sleep. Not drug-induced unconsciousness, but real, restorative sleep. The best we can do is to manage his pain and leave him alone."

"Why did you do this to him?" Castle. *Castle is here.* But his voice is harsh. A little scared. "Was it necessary? Truly?"

Silence.

"*Nazeera.*" It's Stephan.

"It felt necessary," Nazeera says quietly. "At the time."

"You could've just told him, you know." J again. She sounds pissed. "You didn't have to drug him. He would've been fine on the plane if you'd just told him what was going to happen."

"You weren't there, Ella. You don't know. I couldn't risk it. If Anderson had any idea Kenji was on that plane—if Kenji

135

made a *single* sound—we'd all be dead right now. I couldn't trust that he would remain inhumanly still and silent for eight hours, okay? It was the only way."

"But if you really knew him," J says, her anger changing, growing desperate. "If you had any idea what it was like to fight with Kenji by your side, you'd never have thought of him as a liability."

I almost smile.

J always comes through. Always on the team.

"Kenji," she's still saying, "wouldn't have done anything to compromise the mission. He'd have been an asset to you. He could've helped you more than you realize. He—"

Someone clears their throat loudly, and I'm disappointed. I was really enjoying that speech.

"I don't think—" It's one of the twins again. Sara. "I don't think it's helpful to place blame. Not now. And especially not in this instance."

"Actually," Sonya says, and sighs, "we think it was the news about James that pushed him over the edge."

"What?" Nazeera again. "What do you mean?"

Sara: "Kenji loves James. More than most people know. Not everyone realizes how close they are—

"—but we used to see it every day," Sonya says. "Sara and I have been working with James for a while, teaching him how to use his healing powers."

Sonya: "Kenji was always there. He was always checking in. He and James have a special bond."

"And when you're that worried," Sara says, "when you're

that scared, extreme levels of stress can badly injure our immune systems."

Huh. I guess that means my immune system is screwed for life.

Even so, I think I'm feeling better. I'm not only able to distinguish the sounds of their voices, but I'm now realizing that there's a needle in my arm, and it hurts like a bitch.

They must be giving me fluids.

I can't really keep my eyes open yet, but I *can* try to force myself to speak. Unfortunately, my throat is dry. Rough. Sandpaper rough. It feels like way too much work to form complete sentences, but after a minute I manage to croak out two words:

"I'm fine."

"*Kenji.*" I feel Castle rush forward, take my hand. "Thank goodness. We were so worried."

"Okay," I say, but my voice sounds foreign, even to myself. "Like spiders."

The room goes quiet.

"What's he talking about?" someone whispers.

"I think we should let him rest."

Yes. Rest.

So tired.

Can't move anymore. Can't form any more words. I feel like I'm sinking into the mattress.

The voices dissolve, slowly expanding into a mass of unbroken sound that builds into a roaring, painful assault on my ears and then—

Gone.

Quiet.

Darkness.

# NINE

How long has it been?

The air feels cooler, heavier. I try to swallow and, this time, it doesn't hurt. I manage to peek through two slits—remembering something about spiders—and discover that I'm all alone.

I open my eyes a bit more.

I thought I'd wake up in a medical tent or something, but I'm surprised—and relieved, I think—to find that I'm in my own room. All is still. Hushed. Except for one thing: when I listen closely, I can make out the distant, unexpected sound of crickets. I don't think I've heard a cricket in a decade.

Weird.

Anyway, I feel a thousand times better now than I did . . . was it yesterday? I don't know. However long it's been, I can honestly say I'm feeling better now, more like myself. And I know that to be true because I'm suddenly starving. I can't believe I didn't eat that cake when I had the chance. I must've been out of my mind.

I push myself up, onto my elbows.

It's more than a little disorienting to wake up where you didn't fall asleep, but after a few minutes, the room begins to feel familiar. Most of my curtains were pulled closed, but moonlight spills through an inch of uncovered window, casting silvers and shadows across the room. I didn't spend enough time in this tent before things went to hell for me, so the interior is still bare and generic. It doesn't help, of course, that I have none of my things. Everything feels cold. Foreign. All of my belongings are borrowed, even my toothbrush. But when I look out around the room, at the dead monitor stationed near my bed, at the empty IV bag hanging nearby, and at the fresh bandage taped across the new bruise on my forearm, I realize someone must've decided I was okay. That I was going to be okay.

Relief floods through me.

But what do I do about food?

Depending on what time it is, it might be too late to eat; I doubt the dining tent is open at all hours of the night. But right away, my stomach rebels against the thought. It doesn't growl, though, it just hurts. The feeling is familiar, easy to recognize. The sharp, breathtaking pangs of hunger are always the same.

I've known them nearly all my life.

The pain returns again, suddenly, with an insistence I can't ignore, and I realize I have no choice but to scavenge for something. Anything. Even a piece of dry bread. I don't remember the last time I ate a proper meal, now that I think of it. It might've been on the plane, right before we crashed. I wanted to eat dinner that first night, when we arrived at the Sanctuary, but my nerves were so shot that my stomach basically shriveled up and died. I guess I've been starving ever since.

I'm going to fix that.

I push myself all the way up. I need to recalibrate. I've been letting myself lose perspective lately, and I can't afford to do that. There's too much to do. There are too many people depending on me.

James needs me to be better than this.

Besides, I have so much to be grateful for. I know I do. Sometimes I just need to be reminded. So I take a deep, steadying breath in this dark, quiet room and force myself to focus. To remember.

To say, out loud: *I'm grateful.*

For the clothes on my back and the safety of this room. For my friends, my makeshift family, and for what remains of my health and sanity.

I drop my head in my hands and say it. Plant my feet on the floor and say it. And when I've finally managed to pull myself up, breathing hard, breaking a sweat, I brace my hands against the wall and whisper:

"I'm grateful."

I'm going to find James. I'm going to find him and Adam and everyone else. I'm going to make this right. I have to, even if I have to die trying.

I lift my head and step away from the wall, carefully testing my weight on the cold floor. When I realize I feel strong enough to stand on my own, I breathe a sigh of relief. First things first: I need to take a shower.

I grab the hem of my shirt and pull it up, over my head, but just as the collar catches around my face, temporarily blinding me—my arm connects with something.

Someone.

A short, startled gasp is my only confirmation that there's an intruder in my room.

Fear and anger rush through me at the same time, the sensations so overwhelming they leave me suddenly light-headed.

No time for that, though.

I yank the shirt free of my body and toss it to the floor as I spin around, adrenaline rising. I grab the semiautomatic hidden in my pant leg, strapped to the inside of my calf, and pull on my boots faster than I thought humanly possible. Once I've got a firm grip on the gun, my arms fly up, sharp and straight, steadier than I feel inside.

It's just dark enough in here. Too many places to hide.

"Show yourself," I shout. *"Now."*

I don't know exactly what happens next. I can't quite see it, but I can feel it. Wind, curving toward me in a single, fluid arc, and my gun is somehow, impossibly, on the floor. Across the room. I stare at my open, empty hands. Stunned.

I have only a single moment to make a decision.

I pick up a nearby desk chair and slam it, hard, against the wall. One of the wooden legs breaks off easily, and I hold it up, like a bat.

"What do you want?" I say, my hand flexing around the makeshift weapon. "Who sent y—"

I'm kicked from behind.

A heavy, flat boot lands hard between my shoulder blades, knocking me forward with enough force that I lose my balance and my breath. I land on all fours, my head spinning. I'm still too weak. Not nearly fast enough. And I know it.

But when I hear the door swing open, I'm forced upright by something stronger than me—something like loyalty, responsibility for the people I love and need to protect. A slant of moonlight through the open door reveals my gun, still lying on the floor, and I grab it with seconds to spare, somehow getting to the door before it's had a chance to close.

And when I see a glimmer of something in the darkness, I don't hesitate.

I shoot.

I know I've missed when I hear the dull, distant sound of boots, connecting with the ground. My assailant is on the run and moving too fast to have been injured. It's still too dark to see much more than my own feet—the lanterns are out, and the moon is slim—but the quiet is just perfect enough for me to be able to discern careful footfalls in the distance. The closer I get, the more I'm able to track his movements, but the truth is, it's getting harder to hear anything over the sound of my own labored breathing. I have no idea how I'm moving right now. No time to even stop and think about it. My mind is empty save one, single thought:

Apprehend the intruder.

I'm almost afraid to consider who it might be. There's a

very small possibility that this was an accidental intrusion, that maybe it's a civilian who somehow wandered into our camp. But according to what Nouria and Sam said about this place, that sort of thing should be near impossible.

No, it seems a lot more likely that, whoever this is, it's one of Anderson's men. It has to be. He was probably sent here to round up the rest of the supreme kids—maybe going tent to tent in the dead of the night to see who's inside. I'm sure they didn't expect me to be awake.

A sudden, terrifying thought shudders through me, nearly making me stumble. *What if they've already gotten to J?*

I won't let that happen.

I have no idea how anyone—even one of Anderson's men—was able to penetrate the Sanctuary, but if that's where we are, then this is a matter of life and death. I have no idea what happened while I was half-dead in my room, but things must've escalated in my absence. I need to catch this piece of shit, or all our lives could be at risk. And if Anderson gets what he wants tonight, he'll have no reason to keep James and Adam alive anymore. If they're even still alive.

I have to do this. It doesn't matter how weak I feel. I have no choice, not really.

I steel myself, pushing harder, my legs and lungs burning from the effort. Whoever this is, they're perfectly trained. It's hard to admit my own shortcomings, but I can't deny that the only reason I've made it this far is because of the hour—it's so eerily quiet right now that even delicate noises feel loud. And this guy, whoever he is, knows how to run fast, and seemingly forever, without making much sound. If we were anywhere else, at any other time, I'm not sure I'd be able to track him.

But I've got rage and indignation on my side.

When we enter a thick, suffocating stretch of forest, I decide I really, really hate this guy. The moonlight doesn't quite penetrate here, which will make it nearly impossible to spot him, even if I get close enough. But I know I'm gaining on him when our breaths seem to sync up, our footfalls finding a rhythm. He must sense this, too, because I feel him power through, picking up speed with an agility that leaves me in awe. I'm giving this all I've got, but apparently this guy was just having fun. Going for a stroll.

Jesus.

I've got no choice but to play dirty.

I'm not good enough to shoot, while running, at a moving target I can't see—I'm not Warner, for God's sake—so my childish backup plan will have to suffice.

I chuck the gun. Hard. Give it everything I've got.

It's a clean throw, solid. All I need is a stumble. A single, infinitesimal moment of hesitation. Anything to give me an edge.

And when I hear it—a brief, surprised intake of air—

I launch myself forward with a cry, and tackle him to the ground.

# TEN

"What . . . the hell?"

I must be hallucinating. I *better* be hallucinating.

"I'm sorry, I'm sorry, oh my God, I'm so sorry—"

I try to push myself up, but I threw myself forward with everything I had, and I nearly knocked myself out in the process. I've barely got enough strength left to stand. Still, I manage to shift myself a little to the side and, when I feel the damp grass against my skin, I remember that I'm not wearing a shirt.

I swear loudly.

This night could not possibly get worse.

But then, in the space of half a second, my mind catches up to my body and the force of understanding—of realization—is so intense that it nearly blinds me. Anger, hot and wild, surges through me, and it's enough to propel me up and away from her. I stumble backward, onto the ground, and hit my head against a tree trunk.

"Son of a—" I cut myself off with an angry cry.

Nazeera scrambles backward.

She's still planted on the ground, her eyes wild, her hair loose, coming free of its tie. I've never seen her look so terrified. I've never seen her look so paralyzed. And something about the pained look in her eyes takes the edge off my anger.

Just the edge.

*"Are you out of your fucking mind?"* I cry. "What the hell are you doing?"

"Oh my God, I'm so sorry," she says, and drops her face in her hands.

"You're sorry?" I'm still shouting. "You're *sorry*? I could've *killed* you."

And even then, even in this horrible, unbelievable moment, she has the audacity to look me in the eye and say: "I doubt that."

I swear to God, my eyes go so wide with rage I think they split my face open. I have no idea what I'm supposed to do with this woman.

No fucking clue.

"I—I don't even—" I flounder, fighting for the right words. "There are so many reasons why you should be, like, shipped off on a one-way ticket to the moon right now, I don't even know where to start." I run my hands through my hair, grabbing fistfuls. "What were you *thinking*? Why—why—" And then, suddenly, something occurs to me. A cold, sick feeling gathers in my chest and I drop my hands. Look at her.

"Nazeera," I say quietly. "Why were you in my room?"

She pulls her knees to her chest. Closes her eyes. And only when I can no longer see her face—when she presses her forehead to her knees—does she say: "I honestly think this might be the most embarrassing moment of my entire life."

My muscles go slack. I stare at her, stunned, confused, angrier than I've been in years. "I don't understand."

She shakes her head. Just keeps shaking her head. "You weren't supposed to wake up," she says. "I thought you'd sleep through the night. I just wanted to check on you—I wanted to make sure you were okay because it was all my fault and I felt—I felt so *awful*—"

I open my mouth. No words come out.

"—but then you woke up and I didn't know what to do," she says, finally lifting her head. "I didn't—I didn't—"

"Bullshit," I say, cutting her off. "*Bullshit* you didn't know what to do. If you were really in my room because you were worried about my welfare, you could've just said hi to me, like a normal person. You'd say something like, 'Oh, hello Kenji, it's me, Nazeera! I'm just here to make sure you're not dead!' and I'd say 'Gee, thanks, Nazeera, that's so nice of you!' and you'd—"

"It's not that simple," she says, shaking her head again. "It's just— It wasn't that simple—"

"No," I say angrily. "You're right. It's not that simple."

I get to my feet, dust off my hands. "You want to know why? You want to know why it's not that simple? Because your story doesn't add up. You say you came into my room to check on me—because you claim to be concerned about my health—but then, the first chance you get, you kick a sick man in the back, knock him to the floor, and then make him chase you through the woods *with no shirt on*.

"No," I say, rage building inside me again. "No way. You don't give a shit about my health. You"—I point at her—"you're up to something. First the drugs on the plane, and now this. You're trying to *kill* me, Nazeera, and I don't understand why.

"What happened? You didn't finish the job the first time? You came back to make sure I was dead? Was that it?"

Slowly, she gets to her feet, but she can't meet my eyes.

Her silence is driving me crazy.

"I want answers," I cry, shaking with fury. "Right now. I want to know what the hell you're doing. I want to know why you're here. I want to know who you're working for." And then, practically screaming the words: *"And I want to know why you were in my goddamn room tonight."*

"Kenji," she says quietly. "I'm sorry. I'm not good at this. That's all I can tell you. I'm sorry."

I'm so shocked by her gall I actually flinch in response.

"Truly, I'm sorry," she says again. She's backing away from me. Slowly, but still—I've seen this girl run. "Let me just go die of humiliation somewhere else, okay? I'm so sorry."

"*Stop.*"

She goes suddenly still.

I try to steady my breathing. Can't. My chest is still heaving when I say, "Just tell me the truth."

"*I told you the truth,*" she says, anger flaring in her eyes. "I'm not good at this, Kenji. I'm not good at this."

149

"What are you talking about? Of course you're good at this. Murdering people is, like, your life's work."

She laughs, but she sounds a little hysterical. "Do you remember," she says, "when I told you that this could never work?" She makes that familiar motion, that gesture between our bodies. "Do you remember that day?"

Something unconscious, something primal I can't control, sends a sharp needle of heat through my body. Even now.

"Yes," I say. "I remember."

"This," she says, waving her arms around. "This is what I was talking about."

I frown. I feel like I've lost track of the conversation. "I don't . . ." I frown again. "What are you talking about?"

"*This,*" she says, fury edging into her voice. "This. *This.* You don't understand. I don't know how to— I just don't do this, okay? Ever. I tried to tell you that day that I don't— But now—" She cuts herself off with a sharp shake of her head. Turns away. "Please don't make me say it."

"Say what?"

"That you're—" She stops. "That this—"

I wait, and wait, and still, she says nothing.

"I *what*? This *what*?"

Finally, she sighs. Meets my eyes. "You were my first kiss."

# ELEVEN

I could've spent years trying to figure out what she was about to say to me, and I never would've gotten it right.

Never.

I'm beyond stunned. Beyond dumbfounded.

And all I can come up with is—

"You're lying."

She shakes her head.

"But—"

She keeps shaking her head.

"I don't understand."

"I like you," she says quietly. "A lot."

Something flashes through me—something terrifying. A rush of feeling. A lick of fire. *Joy.* And then denial, denial, fast and hard.

"Bullshit."

"Not bullshit," she whispers.

"But you've been trying to kill me."

"No." She hangs her head. "I've been trying to show you I care."

I can only stare at her, bewildered.

"I gave you a slightly stronger dose of that drug because I was so worried you'd wake up on the plane and get yourself murdered," she says. "I was in your room tonight because I wanted to make sure you were okay, but when you woke up I got nervous and disappeared. And then you started talking, and the things you said were so beautiful that I just"—she shakes her head—"I don't know. The truth is, I don't have an excuse. I stayed because I wanted to stay. I stayed and I watched you like a creep, and when you caught me I was so mortified I nearly killed you for it."

She covers her face with her hands.

"I have no idea what I'm doing," she says, her words so small and quiet I have to step closer to hear them. "I've been prepared for literally every single other high-stress situation life can throw my way, but I have no idea how to properly reciprocate positive emotion. I was never shown how. Never taught how to do it. And, as a result, I've avoided it altogether."

Finally, she meets my eyes.

"I've always avoided doing things I know I'll be bad at," she says. "And with this— Relationships? Physical intimacy? I just . . . don't. Ever. With anyone. It's too messy. Too confusing. There's too much code, too much garbage to filter and decipher. Besides, most of the people I meet are either assholes or cowards or both. They're rarely genuine. They never say what they're really thinking. And they all lie to my face." She sighs. "Except for you, of course."

"Nazeera—"

"Please," she says softly. "This is so humiliating. And if it's all right with you, I really don't want to drag this conversation out any more than I absolutely have to. But I swear—after today—I won't come near you again. I'll keep my distance. I promise. I'm so sorry I hurt you. I never meant to kick you that hard."

And she leaves.

She turns on her heel and stalks off, and I'm seized by something, something that feels a lot like panic when I say—

"Wait!"

She freezes.

I run after her, grab her by the waist and spin her around, and she looks surprised, and then uncertain, and I say:

"Why me?"

She goes still. "What do you mean?"

"I mean— That day, when you kissed me. You chose me that day, didn't you? For your first kiss."

After a moment, she nods.

"Why?" I say. "Why'd you choose me?"

All of a sudden, her eyes go soft. The tension in her shoulders disappears. "Because," she says quietly, "I think you might be the best person I've ever met."

"Oh."

I take a deep, uneven breath, but it's not getting me enough oxygen. Feeling is flooding through me, so fast and hot I can't even remember that I'm freezing.

I think I'm dreaming.

God, I hope I'm not dreaming.

"Kenji?"

*Say something, dumbass.*

Nope.

She sighs, the sound filling the silence. And then she looks down, at the ground between us. "I'm really, really sorry I kicked you like that. Are you okay?"

I shrug, and then wince. "I probably won't be able to walk in the morning."

She looks up. There's something like laughter in her eyes.

"It's not funny," I say, but I'm starting to smile, too. "That was horrible. And— Jesus," I say, feeling suddenly sick. "I tried to shoot you for it."

She laughs.

*Laughs*, like I just made a joke.

"I'm serious, Nazeera. I could've killed you."

Her smile fades when she realizes I'm serious. And then she looks at me, really looks at me. "That's not possible."

I roll my eyes, but I can't help but crack a smile at her certainty.

"You know," she says softly, "I think there was a part of me that was really hoping you'd catch me."

"Yeah?"

"Yeah," she whispers. "Otherwise—why didn't I just fly away?"

I take a second to let that sink in.

And then—

*Damn.*

She's right. I never stood a chance against this girl.

"Hey," I say.

"Yeah?"

"You're completely insane, you know that?"

"Yeah," she says, and sighs.

And somehow, impossibly—

I'm smiling.

Carefully, I reach out, grazing her cheek with the tips of my fingers. She trembles under my touch. Closes her eyes.

My heart stops.

"Nazeera, I—"

A wild, piercing, bloodcurdling scream brings the moment to a halt.

# TWELVE

Nazeera and I share a split-second glance before we're running again. I follow her through the woods, toward the source of the scream, but almost as quickly as it came—the world goes quiet. We rush to a sudden, confused stop, nearly falling over in the process. Nazeera turns to look at me, her eyes wide, but she's not seeing me, not really.

She's waiting. Listening.

Suddenly, she straightens. I don't know what she heard, because I heard nothing. But I've already realized that this girl is way out of my league; I have no idea what other skills she possesses. No idea what else she's capable of. But I do know that there's no point doubting her mind. Not when it comes to shit like this.

So when she starts running again, I'm right behind her.

I realize we're heading back toward the beginning, to the entrance of Nouria's camp, when three more screams pierce the night. Then, suddenly—

At least a hundred more.

And then I realize where Nazeera is headed. *Out.* Out of the Sanctuary, into unprotected land where we could too easily be found, captured, and killed. I hesitate, old doubts asking me if I'm crazy to trust her—

"Stealth, Kenji— *Now*—"

And she disappears. I take a deep breath and follow suit.
It's not long before I understand.

Outside of the protection of the Sanctuary, the screams intensify, rising and multiplying in the darkness. Except that it's not dark, not here. Not exactly. The sky is split, darkness and light melting together, clouds falling sideways, trees bending, flickering, bending and flickering. The earth beneath us has begun to pucker and crack, divots forming midair, puncturing nothing and everything. And then—

The horizon moves.

Suddenly the sun is underneath us, searing and blinding and fracturing light like lightning as it skids along the grass.

Just as quickly, the horizon swings back into place.

The scene is beyond surreal.

I can't process. Can't digest. People are trying to run but can't. They're too overcome. Too confused. They make it only a few feet before something changes again, before they're screaming again, before everyone is plunged into darkness, into light, into darkness, into light.

Nazeera materializes at my side. We've pulled back our invisibility. It seems obvious now that there's no longer any point in stealth. Not here. Not in this.

And when Nazeera turns abruptly and starts running, I already know she's heading back to camp.

We have to tell the others.

Except, as it turns out, they already know.

I see her before we've made it back. Right outside the entrance, backlit by chaos:

*Juliette.*

She's on her knees, her hands clamped around her temples. Her face is a picture of pure agony, and Warner is crouching beside her, pale and terrified, his hands on her shoulders, shouting something I can't hear.

And then—

She screams.

*Not again*, I think. Please, God, not again.

But it's different this time. This time, the scream is aimed inward; it's an expression of pain, of horror, of travesty.

And this time, when she screams, she says a single, unmistakable sentence:

"*Emmaline*," she screams. "Please don't do this—"

Keep reading for a sneak peek at *Restore Me,*
the fourth book in the SHATTER ME series.

# JULIETTE

I don't wake up screaming anymore. I do not feel ill at the sight of blood. I do not flinch before firing a gun.

I will never again apologize for surviving.

And yet—

I'm startled at once by the sound of a door slamming open. I silence a gasp, spin around, and, by force of habit, rest my hand on the hilt of a semiautomatic hung from a holster at my side.

"J, we've got a serious problem."

Kenji is staring at me—eyes narrowed—his hands on his hips, T-shirt taut across his chest. This is angry Kenji. Worried Kenji. It's been sixteen days since we took over Sector 45—since I crowned myself the supreme commander of The Reestablishment—and it's been quiet. Unnervingly so. Every day I wake up, filled with half terror, half exhilaration, anxiously awaiting the inevitable missives from enemy nations who would challenge my authority and wage war against us—and now, finally, it seems that moment has arrived. So I take a deep breath, crack my neck, and look Kenji in the eye.

"Tell me."

He presses his lips together. Looks up at the ceiling. "So, okay—the first thing you need to know is that this isn't my fault, okay? I was just trying to help."

I falter. Frown. "What?"

"I mean, I knew his punkass was a major drama queen, but this is just beyond ridiculous—"

"I'm sorry—what?" I take my hand off my gun; feel my body unclench. "Kenji, what are you talking about? This isn't about the war?"

"The war? What? J, are you not paying attention? Your boyfriend is having a freaking conniption right now and you need to go handle his ass before I do."

I exhale, irritated. "Are you serious? *Again* with this nonsense? Jesus, Kenji." I unlatch the holster from my back and toss it on the bed behind me. "What did you do this time?"

"See?" Kenji points at me. "See—why are you so quick to judge, huh, princess? Why assume that *I* was the one who did something wrong? Why me?" He crosses his arms against his chest, lowers his voice. "And you know, I've been meaning to talk to you about this for a while, actually, because I really feel that, as supreme commander, you can't be showing preferential treatment like this, but clearly—"

Kenji goes suddenly still.

At the creak of the door Kenji's eyebrows shoot up; a soft click and his eyes widen; a muted rustle of movement and suddenly the barrel of a gun is pressed against the back of his head. Kenji stares at me, his lips making no sound as he mouths the word *psychopath* over and over again.

The psychopath in question winks at me from where he's standing, smiling like he couldn't possibly be holding a gun to the head of our mutual friend. I manage to suppress a laugh.

"Go on," Warner says, still smiling. "Please tell me exactly how she's failed you as a leader."

"*Hey—*" Kenji's arms fly up in mock surrender. "I never said she failed at anything, okay? And you are clearly over-react—"

Warner knocks Kenji on the side of the head with the weapon. "Idiot."

Kenji spins around. Yanks the gun out of Warner's hand. "What the hell is wrong with you, man? I thought we were cool."

"We were," Warner says icily. "Until you touched my *hair*."

"You asked me to give you a haircut—"

"I said nothing of the sort! I asked you to trim the edges!"

"And that's what I did."

"*This,*" Warner says, spinning around so I might inspect the damage, "is not trimming the edges, you incompetent moron—"

I gasp. The back of Warner's head is a jagged mess of uneven hair; entire chunks have been buzzed off.

Kenji cringes as he looks over his handiwork. Clears his throat. "Well," he says, shoving his hands in his pockets. "I mean—whatever, man, beauty is subjective—"

Warner aims another gun at him.

"Hey!" Kenji shouts. "I am not here for this abusive relationship, okay?" He points at Warner. "I did not sign up for this shit!"

Warner glares at him and Kenji retreats, backing out of the room before Warner has another chance to react; and then, just as I let out a sigh of relief, Kenji pops his head back into the doorway and says

"I think the cut looks cute, actually"

and Warner slams the door in his face.

Welcome to my brand-new life as supreme commander of The Reestablishment.

Warner is still facing the closed door as he exhales, his shoulders losing their tension as he does, and I'm able to see even more clearly the mess Kenji has made. Warner's thick, gorgeous, golden hair—a defining feature of his beauty—chopped up by careless hands.

A disaster.

"Aaron," I say softly.

He hangs his head.

"Come here."

He turns around, looking at me out of the corner of his eye like he's done something to be ashamed of. I clear the guns off the bed and make room for him beside me. He sinks into the mattress with a sad sigh.

"I look hideous," he says quietly.

I shake my head, smiling, and touch his cheek. "Why did you let him cut your hair?"

Warner looks up at me then; his eyes round and green and perplexed. "You told me to spend time with him."

I laugh out loud. "So you let Kenji cut your hair?"

"I didn't let him *cut* my hair," he says, scowling. "It was"—he hesitates—"it was a gesture of camaraderie. It was an act of trust I'd seen practiced among my soldiers. In any case," he says, turning away, "it's not as though I have any experience building friendships."

"Well," I say. "We're friends, aren't we?"

At this, he smiles.

"And?" I nudge him. "That's been good, hasn't it? You're learning to be nicer to people."

"Yes, well, I don't want to be nicer to people. It doesn't suit me."

"I think it suits you beautifully," I say, beaming. "I love it when you're nice."

"You would say that." He almost laughs. "But being kind does not come naturally to me, love. You'll have to be patient with my progress."

I take his hand in mine. "I have no idea what you're talking about. You're perfectly kind to me."

Warner shakes his head. "I know I promised I would make an effort to be nicer to your friends—and I will continue to make that effort—but I hope I've not led you to believe I'm capable of an impossibility."

"What do you mean?"

"Only that I hope I won't disappoint you. I might, if pressed, be able to generate some degree of warmth, but you must know that I have no interest in treating anyone the way I treat you. *This*," he says, touching the air between us, "is an exception to a very hard rule." His eyes are on my lips now; his hand has moved to my neck. "*This*," he says softly, "is very, very unusual."

I stop

stop breathing, talking, thinking—

He's hardly touched me and my heart is racing; memories crash over me, scalding me in waves: the weight of his body against mine; the taste of his skin; the heat of his touch and his sharp gasps for air and the things he's said to me only in the dark.

Butterflies invade my veins, and I force them out.

This is still so new, his touch, his skin, the scent of him, so new, so new and so incredible—

He smiles, tilts his head; I mimic the movement and with one soft intake of air his lips part and I hold still, my lungs flung to the floor, fingers feeling for his shirt and for what comes next when he says

"I'll have to shave my head, you know"

and pulls away.

I blink and he's still not kissing me.

"And it is my very sincere hope," he says, "that you will still love me when I return."

And then he's up up and away and I'm counting on one hand the number of men I've killed and marveling at how little it's done to help me hold it together in Warner's presence.

I nod once as he waves good-bye, collect my good sense from where I left it, and fall backward onto the bed, head spinning, the complications of war and peace heavy on my mind.

I did not think it would be *easy* to be a leader, exactly, but I do think I thought it would be easier than this:

I am racked with doubt in every moment about the decisions I have made. I am infuriatingly surprised every time a soldier follows my lead. And I am growing more terrified that we—that *I*—will have to kill many, many more before this world is settled. Though I think it's the silence, more than anything else, that's left me shaken.

It's been sixteen days.

I've given speeches about what's to come, about our plans for the future; we've held memorials for the lives lost in battle and we're making good on promises to implement change. Castle, true to his word, is already hard at work, trying to address issues with farming, irrigation, and, most urgent, how best to transition the civilians out of the compounds. But this will be work done in stages; it will be a slow and careful build—a fight for the earth that may take a century. I think we all understand that. And if it were only the civilians I had to worry about, I would not worry so much. But I worry because I know too well that nothing can be done to fix this world if we spend the next several decades at war within it.

Even so, I'm prepared to fight.

It's not what I want, but I'll gladly go to war if it's what we need to do to make a change. I just wish it were that simple. Right now, my biggest problem is also the most confusing:

Wars require enemies, and I can't seem to find any.

In the sixteen days since I shot Anderson in the forehead I have faced zero opposition. No one has tried to arrest me. No other supreme commanders have challenged me. Of the 554 remaining sectors on this continent alone, not a single one has defected, declared war, or spoken ill of me. No one has protested; the people have not rioted. For some reason, The Reestablishment is playing along.

Playing pretend.

And it deeply, deeply unnerves me.

We're in a strange stalemate, stuck in neutral when I desperately want to be doing more. More for the people of Sector 45, for North America, and for the world as a whole. But this strange quiet has thrown all of us off-balance. We were so sure that, with Anderson dead, the other supreme commanders would rise up—that they'd command their armies to destroy us—to destroy *me*. Instead, the leaders of the world have made our insignificance clear: they're ignoring us as they would an annoying fly, trapping us under glass where we're free to buzz around, banging broken wings against the walls for only as long as the oxygen lasts. Sector 45 has been left to do as it pleases; we've been allowed autonomy and the authority to revise the infrastructure of our sector with no interference. Everywhere else—and everyone else—is pretending as though nothing in the world has changed. Our revolution occurred in a vacuum. Our subsequent victory has been reduced to something so small it might not even exist.

*Mind games.*

Castle is always visiting, advising. It was his suggestion that I be proactive—that I take the upper hand. Instead of waiting around, anxious and defensive, I should reach out, he said. I should make my presence known. Stake a claim, he said. Take a seat at the table. And attempt to form alliances before launching assaults. Connect with the five other supreme commanders around the world.

Because I may speak for North America—but what of the rest of the world? What of South America? Europe? Asia? Africa? Oceania?

Host an international conference of leaders, he said.

Talk.

Aim for peace first, he said.

"They must be dying of curiosity," Castle said to me. "A seventeen-year-old girl taking over North America? A teenage girl killing Anderson and declaring herself ruler of this continent? Ms. Ferrars—you must know that you have great leverage at the moment! Use it to your advantage!"

"Me?" I said, stunned. "How do I have leverage?"

Castle sighed. "You certainly are brave for your age, Ms. Ferrars, but I'm sorry to see your youth so inextricably tied to inexperience. I will try to put it plainly: you have superhuman strength, nearly invincible skin, a lethal touch, only seventeen years to your name, and you have single-handedly felled the despot of this nation. And yet you doubt that you might be capable of intimidating the world?"

I cringed.

"Old habits, Castle," I said quietly. "Bad habits. You're

11

right, of course. Of course you're right."

He leveled me with a straight stare. "You must understand that unanimous, collective silence from your enemies is no act of coincidence. They've certainly been in touch with one another—they've certainly agreed to this approach—because they're waiting to see what you do next." He shook his head. "They are awaiting your next move, Ms. Ferrars. I implore you to make it a good one."

So I'm learning.

I did as he suggested and three days ago I sent word through Delalieu and contacted the five other supreme commanders of The Reestablishment. I invited them to join me here, in Sector 45, for a conference of international leaders next month.

Just fifteen minutes before Kenji barged into my room, I'd received my first RSVP.

Oceania said yes.

And I'm not sure what that means.

# WARNER

I've not been myself lately.

The truth is I've not been myself for what feels like a long time, so much so that I've begun to wonder whether I ever really knew. I stare, unblinking, into the mirror, the din of buzzing hair clippers echoing through the room. My face is only dimly reflected in my direction, but it's enough for me to see that I've lost weight. My cheeks are hollow; my eyes, wider; my cheekbones more pronounced. My movements are both mournful and mechanical as I shear off my own hair, the remnants of my vanity falling at my feet.

My father is dead.

I close my eyes, steeling myself against the unwelcome strain in my chest, the clippers still humming in my clenched fist.

*My father is dead.*

It's been just over two weeks since he was killed, shot twice in the forehead by someone I love. She was doing me a kindness by killing him. She was braver than I'd ever been, pulling the trigger when I never could. He was a monster. He deserved worse.

And still—

*This pain.*

I take in a tight breath and blink open my eyes, grateful for the time to be alone; grateful, somehow, for the opportunity to tear asunder something, anything from my flesh. There's a strange catharsis in this.

*My mother is dead*, I think, as I drag the electric blade

across my skull. *My father is dead*, I think, as the hair falls to the floor. Everything I was, everything I did, everything I am, was forged from the twins of their action and inaction.

Who am I, I wonder, in their absence?

Shorn head, blade switched off, I rest my palms against the edge of the vanity and lean in, still trying to catch a glimpse of the man I've become. I feel old and unsettled, my heart and mind at war. The last words I ever spoke to my father—

"Hey."

My heart speeds up as I spin around; I'm affecting nonchalance in an instant. "Hi," I say, forcing my limbs to slow, to be steady as I dust errant strands of hair from my shoulders.

She's looking at me with big eyes, beautiful and worried.

I remember to smile. "How do I look? Not too horrible, I hope."

"Aaron," she says quietly. "Are you okay?"

"I'm fine," I say, and glance again in the mirror. I run a hand over the soft/spiky half inch of hair I have left and wonder at how the cut manages to makes me look harsher—and colder—than before. "Though I confess I don't really recognize myself," I add aloud, attempting a laugh. I'm standing in the middle of the bathroom wearing nothing but boxer briefs. My body has never been leaner, the sharp lines of muscle never more defined; and the rawness of my body is now paired with the rough cut of my hair in a way that feels almost uncivilized—and so unlike me that I have to look away.

Juliette is now right in front of me.

Her hands settle on my hips and pull me forward; I trip a little as I follow her lead. "What are you doing?" I begin to say, but when I meet her eyes I find tenderness and concern. Something thaws inside of me. My shoulders relax and I reel her in, drawing in a deep breath as I do.

"When will we talk about it?" she says against my chest. "All of it? Everything that's happened—"

I flinch.

"Aaron."

"I'm okay," I lie to her. "It's just hair."

"You know that's not what I'm talking about."

I look away. Stare at nothing. We're both quiet a moment. It's Juliette who finally breaks the silence.

"Are you upset with me?" she whispers. "For shooting him?"

My body stills.

Her eyes widen.

"No—*no*." I say the words too quickly, but I mean them. "No, of course not. It's not that."

Juliette sighs.

"I'm not sure you're aware of this," she says finally, "but it's okay to mourn the loss of your father, even if he was a terrible person. You know?" She peers up at me. "You're not a robot."

I swallow back the lump growing in my throat and gently extricate myself from her arms. I kiss her on the cheek and linger there, against her skin, for only a second. "I need to take a shower."

She looks heartbroken and confused, but I don't know what else to do. It's not that I don't love her company, it's just that right now I'm desperate for solitude and I don't know how else to find it.

So I shower. I take baths. I go for long walks.

I tend to do this a lot.

When I finally come to bed she's already asleep.

I want to reach for her, to pull her soft, warm body against my own, but I feel paralyzed. This horrible half-grief has made me feel complicit in darkness. I worry that my sadness will be interpreted as an endorsement of his choices—of his very existence—and in this matter I don't want to be misunderstood, so I cannot admit that I grieve him, that I care at all for the loss of this monstrous man who raised me. And in the absence of healthy action I remain frozen, a sentient stone in the wake of my father's death.

*Are you upset with me? For shooting him?*

I hated him.

I hated him with a violent intensity I've never since experienced. But the fire of true hatred, I realize, cannot exist without the oxygen of affection. I would not hurt so much, or hate so much, if I did not care.

And it is this, my unrequited affection for my father, that has always been my greatest weakness. So I lie here, marinating in a sorrow I can never speak of, while regret consumes my heart.

I am an orphan.

"Aaron?" she whispers, and I'm pulled back to the present.

"Yes, love?"

She moves in a sleepy, sideways motion, and nudges my arm with her head. I can't help but smile as I open up to make room for her against me. She fills the void quickly, pressing her face into my neck as she wraps an arm around my waist. My eyes close as if in prayer. My heart restarts.

"I miss you," she says. It's a whisper I almost don't catch.

"I'm right here," I say, gently touching her cheek. "I'm right here, love."

But she shakes her head. Even as I pull her closer, even as she falls back asleep, she shakes her head.

And I wonder if she's not wrong.

Read on for a preview of *A Very Large Expanse
of Sea*, the National Book Award–longlisted
contemporary debut by Tahereh Mafi.

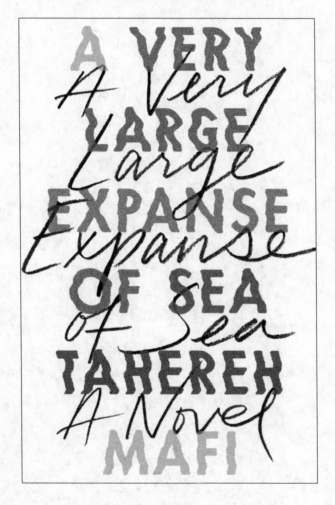

## ONE

We always seemed to be moving, always for the better, always to make our lives better, whatever. I couldn't keep up with the emotional whiplash. I'd attended so many elementary schools and middle schools I couldn't keep their names straight anymore but this, this switching high schools all the time thing was really starting to make me want to die. This was my third high school in less than two years and my life seemed suddenly to comprise such a jumble of bullshit every day that sometimes I could hardly move my lips. I worried that if I spoke or screamed my anger would grip both sides of my open mouth and rip me in half.

So I said nothing.

It was the end of August, all volatile heat and the occasional breeze. I was surrounded by starched backpacks and stiff denim and kids who smelled like fresh plastic. They seemed happy.

I sighed and slammed my locker shut.

For me, today was just another first day of school in another new city, so I did what I always did when I showed up at a new school: I didn't look at people. People were always looking at me, and when I looked back they often took it as an invitation to speak to me, and when they spoke to me they nearly always said something offensive or stupid or both and I'd decided a long time ago that it was easier to pretend they just didn't exist.

I'd managed to survive the first three classes of the day without major incident, but I was still struggling to navigate the school itself. My next class seemed to be on the other side of campus, and I was trying to figure out where I was—cross-checking room numbers against my new class schedule—when the final bell rang. In the time it took my stunned self to glance up at the clock, the masses of students around me had disappeared. I was suddenly alone in a long, empty hallway, my printed schedule now crumpled in one fist. I squeezed my eyes shut and swore under my breath.

When I finally found my next class I was seven minutes late. I pushed open the door, the hinges slightly squeaking, and students turned around in their seats. The teacher stopped talking, his mouth still caught around a sound, his face frozen between expressions.

He blinked at me.

I averted my eyes, even as I felt the room contract around me. I slid into the nearest empty seat and said nothing. I took a notebook out of my bag. Grabbed a pen. I was hardly breathing, waiting for the moment to pass, waiting for people to turn away, waiting for my teacher to start talking again when he suddenly cleared his throat and said—

"Anyway, as I was saying: our syllabus includes quite a bit of required reading, and those of you who are new here"—he hesitated, glanced at the roster in his hands—"might be unaccustomed to our school's intense and, ah, highly demanding curriculum." He stopped. Hesitated again. Squinted at the paper in his hands.

And then, as if out of nowhere, he said, "Now—forgive me if I'm saying this incorrectly—but is it—*Sharon*?" He looked up, looked me directly in the eye.

I said, "It's Shirin."

Students turned to look at me again.

"Ah." My teacher, Mr. Webber, didn't try to pronounce my name again. "Welcome."

I didn't answer him.

"So." He smiled. "You understand that this is an honors English class."

I hesitated. I wasn't sure what he was expecting me to say to such an obvious statement. Finally, I said, "Yes?"

He nodded, then laughed, and said, "Sweetheart, I think you might be in the wrong class."

I wanted to tell him not to call me *sweetheart*. I wanted to tell him not to talk to me, ever, as a general rule. Instead, I said, "I'm in the right class," and held up my crumpled schedule.

Mr. Webber shook his head, even as he kept smiling. "Don't worry—this isn't your fault. It happens sometimes with new students. But the ESL office is actually just down the—"

"I'm in the right class, okay?" I said the words more forcefully than I'd intended. "I'm in the right class."

This shit was always happening to me.

It didn't matter how unaccented my English was. It didn't matter that I told people, over and over again, that I was born here, *in America*, that English was my first language, that my cousins in Iran made fun of me for speaking mediocre Farsi with an American accent—it didn't matter. Everyone assumed I was fresh off the boat from a foreign land.

Mr. Webber's smile faltered. "Oh," he said. "Okay."

The kids around me started laughing and I felt my face getting hot. I looked down and opened my blank notebook to a random page, hoping the action would inspire an end to the conversation.

Instead, Mr. Webber held up his hands and said, "Listen—me, personally? I want you to stay, okay? But this is a really advanced class, and even though I'm sure your English is really good, it's still—"

"My English," I said, "isn't *really good*. My English is fucking perfect."

I spent the rest of the hour in the principal's office.

I was given a stern talking-to about the kind of behavior expected of students at this school and warned that, if I was going to be deliberately hostile and uncooperative, maybe this wasn't the school for me. And then I was given detention for using vulgar language in class. The lunch bell rang while the principal was yelling at me, so when he finally let me go I grabbed my things and bolted.

I wasn't in a hurry to get anywhere; I was only looking forward to being away from people. I had two more classes to get through after lunch but I wasn't sure my head could take it; I'd already surpassed my threshold for stupidity for the day.

I was balancing my lunch tray on my lap in a bathroom stall, my head in a viselike grip between my hands, when my phone buzzed. It was my brother.

> what are you doing?
> **eating lunch**
> bullshit. where are you hiding?
> **in the bathroom**
> what? why?
> **what else am i supposed to do for 37 minutes?**
> **stare at people?**

And then he told me to get the hell out of the bathroom and come have lunch with him, apparently the school had already sent out a welcome wagon full of brand-new friends in celebration of his pretty face, and I should join him instead of hiding.

**no thanks**, I typed.

And then I threw my lunch in the trash and hid in the library until the bell rang.

My brother is two years older than me; we'd almost always been in the same school at the same time. But he didn't hate moving like I did; he didn't always suffer when we got to a new city. There were two big differences between me and my brother: first, that he was extremely handsome, and second, that he didn't walk around wearing a metaphorical neon sign nailed to his forehead flashing CAUTION, TERRORIST APPROACHING.

I shit you not, girls lined up to show my brother around the school. He was the good-looking new guy. The interesting boy with an interesting past and an interesting name. The handsome exotic boy all these pretty girls would inevitably use to satisfy their need to experiment and one day rebel against their parents. I'd learned the hard way that I couldn't eat lunch with him and his friends. Every time I showed up, tail between my legs and my pride in the trash, it took all of five seconds for me to realize that the only reason his new lady friends were being nice to me was because they wanted to use me to get to my brother.

I'd rather eat in the toilet.

I told myself I didn't care, but obviously I did. I had to. The news cycle never let me breathe anymore. 9/11 happened last fall, two weeks into my freshman year, and a couple of weeks later two dudes attacked me while I was walking home from school and the worst part—the worst part—was that it took me days to shake off the denial; it took me days to fathom the *why*. I kept hoping the explanation would turn out to be more complex, that there'd turn out to be more than pure, blind hatred to motivate their actions. I wanted there to be some other reason why two strangers would follow me home, some other reason why they'd yank my scarf off my head and try to choke me with it. I didn't understand how anyone could be so violently angry with me for something I hadn't done, so much so that they'd feel justified in assaulting me in broad daylight as I walked down the street.

I didn't *want* to understand it.

But there it was.

I hadn't expected much when we moved here, but I was still sorry to discover that this school seemed no better than my last one. I was stuck in another small town, trapped in another universe populated by the kind of people who'd only ever seen faces like mine on their evening news, and I hated it. I hated the exhausting, lonely months it took to settle into a new school; I hated how long it took for the kids around me to realize I was neither terrifying nor dangerous; I hated the pathetic, soul-sucking effort it took to finally make a single friend brave enough to sit next to me in public. I'd had to relive this awful cycle so many times, at so many different schools, that sometimes I really wanted to put my head through a wall.

All I wanted from the world anymore was to be perfectly unremarkable. I wanted to know what it was like to walk through a room and be stared at by no one. But a single glance around campus deflated any hopes I might've had for blending in.

The student body was, for the most part, a homogenous mass of about two thousand people who were apparently in love with basketball. I'd already walked past dozens of posters—and a massive banner hung over the front doors—celebrating a team that wasn't even in season yet. There were oversize black-and-white numbers taped to hallway walls, signs screaming at passersby to count down the days until the first game of the season.

I had no interest in basketball.

Instead, I'd been counting the number of dipshit things people had said to me today. I'd been holding strong at fourteen until I made my way to my next class and some kid passing me in the hall asked if I wore that thing on my head because I was hiding bombs underneath and I ignored him, and then his friend said that maybe I was secretly bald and I ignored him, and then a third one said that I was probably, actually, a man, and just trying to hide it and finally I told them all to fuck off, even as they congratulated one another on having drummed up these excellent hypotheses. I had no idea what these asswipes looked like because I never glanced in their direction, but I was thinking seventeen, *seventeen*, as I got to my next class way too early and waited, in the dark, for everyone else to show up.

These, the regular injections of poison I was gifted from strangers, were definitely the worst things about wearing a headscarf. But the best thing about it was that my teachers couldn't see me listening to music.

It gave me the perfect cover for my earbuds.

Music made my day so much easier. Walking through the halls at school was somehow easier; sitting alone all the time was easier. I loved that no one could tell I was listening to music and that, because no one knew, I was never asked to turn it off. I'd had multiple conversations with teachers who had no idea I was only half hearing whatever they were saying to me, and for some reason this made me happy. Music seemed to steady me like a second skeleton; I leaned on it when my own bones were too shaken to stand. I always listened to music on the iPod I'd stolen from my brother and, here—as I did last year, when he first bought the thing—I walked to class like I was listening to the soundtrack of my own shitty movie. It gave me an inexplicable kind of hope.

When my last class of the day had finally assembled, I was already watching my teacher on mute. My mind wandered; I kept checking the clock, desperate to escape. Today, the Fugees were filling the holes in my head, and I stared at my pencil case, turning it over and over in my hands. I was really into mechanical pencils. Like, nice ones. I had a small collection, actually, that I'd gotten from an old friend from four moves ago; she'd brought them back for me from Japan and I was mildly obsessed. The pencils were delicate and colorful and glittery and they'd come with a set of adorable erasers and this really cute case with a cartoon picture of a sheep on it, and the sheep said *Do not make light of me just because I am a sheep*, and I'd always thought it was so funny and strange and I was remembering this now, smiling a little, when someone tapped me on the shoulder. Hard.

"What?" I turned around as I said it, speaking too loudly by accident.

Some dude. He looked startled.

"What?" I said quietly, irritated now.

He said something but I couldn't hear him. I tugged the iPod out of my pocket and hit pause.

"Uh." He blinked at me. Smiled, but seemed confused about it. "You're listening to music under there?"

"Can I help you?"

"Oh. No. No, I just bumped your shoulder with my book. By accident. I was trying to say sorry."

"Okay." I turned back around. I hit play on my music again.

The day passed.

People had butchered my name, teachers hadn't known what the hell to do with me, my math teacher looked at my face and gave a five-minute speech to the class about how people who don't love this country should just go back to where they came from and I stared at my textbook so hard it was days before I could get the quadratic equation out of my head.

Not one of my classmates spoke to me, no one but the kid who accidentally assaulted my shoulder with his bio book.

I wished I didn't care.

I walked home that day feeling both relieved and dejected. It took a lot out of me to put up the walls that kept me safe from heartbreak, and at the end of every day I felt so withered by the emotional exertion that sometimes my whole body felt shaky. I was trying to steady myself as I made my way down the quiet stretch of sidewalk that would carry me home—trying to shake this heavy, sad fog from my head—when a car slowed down just long enough for a lady to shout at me that I was in America now, so I should dress like it, and I was just, I don't know, I was so goddamn tired I couldn't even drum up the enthusiasm to be angry, not even as I offered her a full view of my middle finger as she drove away.

*Two and a half more years*, was all I could think.

Two and a half more years until I could get free from this panopticon they called high school, these monsters they called people. I was desperate to escape the institution of idiots. I wanted to go to college, make my own life. I just had to survive until then.

## TWO

My parents were actually pretty great, as far as human beings went. They were proud Iranian immigrants who worked hard, all day, to make my life—and my brother's life—better. Every move we made was to bring us into a better neighborhood, into a bigger house, into a better school district with better options for our future. They never stopped fighting, my parents. Never stopped striving. I knew they loved me. But you have to know, right up front, that they had zero sympathy for what they considered were my unremarkable struggles.

My parents never talked to my teachers. They never called my school. They never threatened to call some other kid's mother because her son threw a rock at my face. People had been shitting on me for having the wrong name/race/religion and socioeconomic status since as far back as I could remember, but my life had been so easy in comparison to my parents' own upbringing that they genuinely couldn't understand why I didn't wake up singing every morning. My dad's personal story was so insane—he'd left home, all alone, for America when he was sixteen—that the part where he was drafted to go to war in Vietnam actually seemed like a highlight. When I was a kid and would tell my mom that people at school were mean to me, she'd pat me on the head and tell me stories about how she'd lived through war and an actual revolution, and when she was fifteen someone cracked open her skull in the middle of the street while her best friend was gutted like a fish so, hey, why don't you just eat your Cheerios and walk it off, you ungrateful American child.

I ate my Cheerios. I didn't talk about it.

I loved my parents, I really did. But I never talked to them about my own pain. It was impossible to compete for sympathy with a mother and father who thought I was lucky to attend a school where the teachers only *said* mean things to you and didn't *actually* beat the shit out of you.

So I never said much anymore.

I'd come home from school and shrug through my parents' many questions about my day. I'd do my homework; I'd keep myself busy. I read a lot of books. It's such a cliché, I know, the lonely kid and her books, but the day my brother walked into my room and chucked a copy of *Harry Potter* at my head and said, "I won this at school, looks like something you'd enjoy," was one of the best days of my life. The few friends I'd made who didn't live exclusively on paper had collapsed into little more than memories and even those were fading fast. I'd lost a lot in our moves—things, stuff, objects—but nothing hurt as much as losing people.

Anyway, I was usually on my own.

My brother, though, he was always busy. He and I used to be close, used to be best friends, but then one day he woke up to discover he was cool and handsome and I was not, that in fact my very existence scared the crap out of people, and, I don't know, we lost touch. It wasn't on purpose. He just always had people to see, things to do, girls to call, and I didn't. I liked my brother, though. Loved him, even. He was a good guy when he wasn't annoying the shit out of me.

I survived the first three weeks at my new school with very little to report. It was unexciting. Tedious. I interacted with people on only the most basic, perfunctory levels, and otherwise spent most of my time listening to music. Reading. Flipping through *Vogue*. I was really into complicated fashion that I could never afford and I spent my weekends scouring thrift stores, trying to find pieces that were reminiscent of my favorite looks from the runway, looks that I would later, in the quiet of my bedroom, attempt to re-create. But I was only mediocre with a sewing machine; I did my best work by hand. Even so, I kept breaking needles and accidentally stabbing myself and showing up to school with too many Band-Aids on my fingers, prompting my teachers to shoot me even weirder looks than usual. Still, it kept me distracted. It was only the middle of September and I was already struggling to give even the vaguest shit about school.

After another exhilarating day at the panopticon I collapsed onto the couch. My parents weren't home from work yet, and I didn't know where my brother was. I sighed, turned on the television, and tugged my scarf off my head. Pulled the ponytail free and ran a hand through my hair. Settled back onto the couch.

There were *Matlock* reruns on TV every afternoon at exactly this hour, and I was not embarrassed to admit out loud that I loved them. I loved *Matlock*. It was a show that was created even before I was born, about a really old, really expensive lawyer named Matlock who solved criminal cases for a ton of money. These days it was popular only with the geriatric crowd, but this didn't bother me. I often felt like a very old person trapped in a young person's body; Matlock was my people. All I needed was a bowl of prunes or a cup of applesauce to finish off the look, and I was beginning to wonder if maybe we had some stashed somewhere in the fridge when I heard my brother come home.

At first I didn't think anything of it. He shouted a hello to the house and I made a noncommittal noise; Matlock was being awesome and I couldn't be bothered to look away.

"Hey—didn't you hear me?"

I popped my head up. Saw my brother's face.

"I brought some friends over," he was saying, and even then I didn't quite understand, not until one of the guys walked into the living room and I stood up so fast I almost fell over.

"*What the hell*, Navid?" I hissed, and grabbed my scarf. It was a comfortable, pashmina shawl that was normally very easy to wear, but I fumbled in the moment, feeling flustered, and somehow ended up shoving it onto my head. The guy just smiled at me.

"Oh—don't worry," he said quickly. "I'm like eighty percent gay."

"That's nice," I said, irritated, "but this isn't about you."

"This is Bijan," Navid said to me, and he could hardly contain his laughter as he nodded at the new guy, who was so obviously Persian I almost couldn't believe it; I didn't think there were other Middle Eastern people in this town. But Navid was now laughing at my face and I realized then that I must've looked ridiculous, standing there with my scarf bunched awkwardly on my head. "Carlos and Jacobi are—"

"Bye."

I ran upstairs.

I spent a few minutes considering, as I paced the length of my bedroom floor, how embarrassing that incident had been. I felt flustered and stupid, caught off guard like that, but I finally decided that though the whole thing was kind of embarrassing, it was not so embarrassing that I could justify hiding up here for hours without food. So I tied my hair back, carefully reassembled myself—I didn't like pinning my scarf in place, so I usually wrapped it loosely around my head, tossing the longer ends over my shoulders—and reemerged.

When I walked into the living room, I discovered the four boys sitting on the couch and eating, what looked like, everything in our pantry. One of them had actually found a bag of prunes and was currently engaged in stuffing them in his mouth.

"Hey." Navid glanced up.

"Hi."

The boy with the prunes looked at me. "So you're the little sister?"

I crossed my arms.

"This is Carlos," Navid said. He nodded at the other guy I hadn't met, this really tall black dude, and said, "That's Jacobi."

Jacobi waved an unenthusiastic hand without even looking in my direction. He was eating all the rosewater nougat my mom's sister had sent her from Iran. I doubted he even knew what it was.

Not for the first time, I was left in awe of the insatiable appetite of teenage boys. It grossed me out in a way I couldn't really articulate. Navid was the only one who wasn't eating anything at the moment; instead, he was drinking one of those disgusting protein shakes.

Bijan looked me up and down and said, "You look better."

I narrowed my eyes at him. "How long are you guys going to be here?"

"Don't be rude," Navid said without looking up. He was

now on his knees, messing with the VCR. "I wanted to show these guys *Breakin'*."

I was more than a little surprised.

*Breakin'* was one of my favorite movies.

I couldn't remember how our obsession started, exactly, but my brother and I had always loved breakdancing videos. Movies about breakdancing; hours-long breakdancing competitions from around the world; whatever, anything. It was a thing we shared—a love of this forgotten sport—that had often brought us together at the end of the day. We'd found this movie, *Breakin'*, at a flea market a few years ago, and we'd watched it at least twenty times already.

"Why?" I said. I sat down in an armchair, curled my legs up underneath me. I wasn't going anywhere. *Breakin'* was one of the few things I enjoyed more than *Matlock*. "What's the occasion?"

Navid turned back. Smiled at me. "I want to start a breakdancing crew."

I stared at him. "Are you serious?"

Navid and I had talked about this so many times before: what it would be like to breakdance—to really learn and perform—but we'd never actually done anything about it. It was something I'd thought about for years.

Navid stood up then. He smiled wider. I knew he could tell I was super excited. "You in?"

"Fuck yeah," I said softly.

My mom walked into the room at that exact moment and whacked me in the back of the head with a wooden spoon.

"*Fosh nadeh*," she snapped. *Don't swear.*

I rubbed the back of my head. "Damn, Ma," I said. "That shit hurt."

She whacked me in the back of the head again.

"*Damn.*"

"Who's this?" she said, and nodded at my brother's new friends.

Navid made quick work of the introductions while my mother took inventory of all that they'd eaten. She shook her head. "*Een chiyeh?*" she said. *What's this?* And then, in English: "This isn't food."

"It's all we had," Navid said to her. Which was sort of true. My parents never, ever bought junk food. We never had chips or cookies lying around. When I wanted a snack my mom would hand me a cucumber.

My mother sighed dramatically at Navid's comment and started scrounging up actual food for us. She then said something in Farsi about how she'd spent all these years teaching her kids how to cook and if she came home from work tomorrow and someone hadn't already made dinner for her we were both going to get our asses kicked—and I was only forty percent sure she was joking.

Navid looked annoyed and I almost started laughing when my mom turned on me and said, "How's school?"

That wiped the smile off my face pretty quickly. But I knew she wasn't asking about my social life. My mom wanted to know about my grades. I'd been in school for less than a month and she was already asking about my grades.

"School's fine," I said.

She nodded, and then she was gone. Always moving, doing, surviving.

I turned to my brother. "So?"

"Tomorrow," he said, "we're going to meet after school."

"And if we get a teacher to supervise," Carlos said, "we could make it an official club on campus."

"Nice." I beamed at my brother.

"I know, right?"

"So, uh, small detail," I said, frowning. "Something I think you might've forgotten—?"

Navid raised an eyebrow.

"Who's going to teach us to breakdance?"

"I am," Navid said, and smiled.

My brother had a bench press in his bedroom that took up half the floor. He found it, disassembled and rusted, next to a dumpster one day, and he hauled it back to one of our old apartments, fixed it, spray-painted it, and slowly amassed a collection of weights to go with it. He dragged that thing around with us everywhere we moved. He loved to train, my brother. To run. To box. He used to take gymnastic classes until they got to be too expensive, and I think he secretly wanted to be a personal trainer. He'd been working out since he was twelve;

he was all muscle and virtually no body fat, and I knew this because he liked to update me on his body-fat percentage on a regular basis. Once, when I'd said, "Good for you," he'd pinched my arm and pursed his lips and said, "Not bad, not bad, but you could stand to build more muscle," and he'd been forcing me to work out with him and his bench press ever since.

So when he said he wanted to teach us how to breakdance, I believed him.

But things were about to get weird.

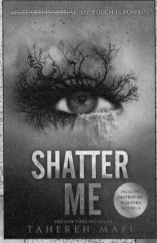

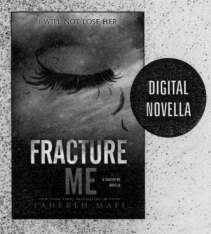

# A girl who's tired of being stereotyped.
# A boy who wants to know who she truly is.

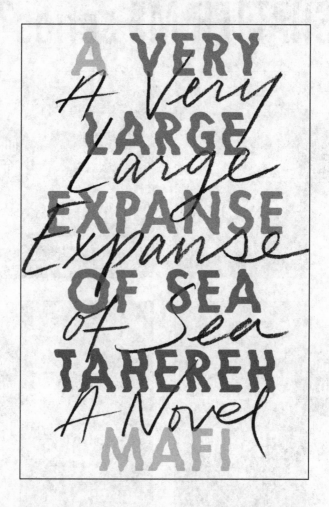

Don't miss this stunning novel from the *New York Times* bestselling author of the SHATTER ME series

**HARPER**
*An Imprint of HarperCollinsPublishers*

www.epicreads.com